The Beginning of Again

By: Jessica Terry

This is a work of fiction. Similarities to real people, places, or events are entirely coincidental.

THE BEGINNING OF AGAIN

First edition. June 5, 2020.

Written by Jessica Terry.

Prologue

E dward could smell the roasted portabellas as soon as he walked through the front door.

"Fuck," he whispered.

The sound of Ronnie's humming wafted through the air along with the aromas of another vegetable-laden meal. Sighing, he set his briefcase by the couch and started for the kitchen, then changed course and went upstairs, delaying greeting his wife. Taking a few minutes to gather himself when he got home from work had become as routine as changing out of his work suit or taking a piss.

Finally, after about twenty minutes, he trudged down the stairs. Ronnie was taking a pot out of the oven when he entered the kitchen. Her smile showed she was glad to see him. He didn't return the gesture. He already knew what she was going to say.

When did you sneak in?

"Hey, when did you sneak in?"

Resisting the urge to roll his eyes, Edward shoved his hands into the pockets of his shorts and shrugged. "A little while ago."

"How come you didn't come speak first?"

"Had to take a piss."

Ronnie frowned disapprovingly. "Edward. Do you have to be so crass?"

"I would think I can say what I want to in my own house."

"You know I don't like it when you talk like that. Show a little respect for me, is all I'm saying."

Edward closed his eyes and took several deep breaths to quell his growing ire. Ronnie was too busy chopping basil to notice.

"Whatever. I'm gonna go watch the news."

"No, dinner is almost ready. Can you grab the rolls and take them to the table?"

"If it's that gluten-free stuff, I don't want any."

"Edward, let's not go through this tonight again, okay? Please just take the rolls to the table."

No kiss, no hug, no interest about how his day went; just instructions.

"Sweetie, you know going meatless is the best thing for you," Ronnie continued as they sat down at the dining room table. "Don't you feel better since we went vegetarian five years ago?"

"*We* didn't go vegetarian, Ronnie. *You* did in college and dragged me along with you after we got married. I still like meat as much as I always did."

She eyed him. "Have you had some today?"

"No, Ronnie." He eyed the bowl in front of him. "What is this?"

"Portobello pot roast. Smells yummy, right?"

"Uh-huh. You know what else would smell yummy? A big ol' slab of babybacks."

"That's not funny."

"Or some pork chops."

"Edward."

"Hell, I'll take a hot dog."

"Stop it!" Ronnie slapped a hand on the table. "You see how you're naming some of the unhealthiest kinds of meats instead of chicken or turkey, or even fish? Since you don't care about your health, I have to."

"Just because I...you know what? Forget it." It was the same argument almost every night and Edward was getting tired of it. He was getting tired of all of this. He just picked up his spoon and began eating.

Taking this as him conceding, Ronnie grinned triumphantly. "It's all because I love you, sweetie."

"Right."

They continued eating in relative silence. Ronnie made conversation that Edward only half listened to. His mind was on other things.

"I was thinking this weekend we could finally clean out all of the closets upstairs," Ronnie suggested. "We've been putting it off forever."

"Actually, I wanted us to go to the Hawks game Saturday night. They're playing the Magic."

"I thought Magic retired years ago."

Edward blinked. "The *Orlando* Magic, Ronnie. Not Magic Johnson. He's in his fifties."

"Oh. Well what about the closets?"

"I don't care about the closets, Ronnie. I want us to have fun, for once, and not spend our weekends doing some boring domestic shit that only you care about."

Ronnie gasped. "Edward!"

"What? Every time I suggest we do something together, you come up with some excuse why we can't do it. Yet if I don't want to do what *you* want, I'm the worst husband ever."

"You're exaggerating."

"I'm not and you know it."

"Edward, come on. You know I don't like sports. Why would you even suggest something you know I don't like?"

"Probably the same way you keep making stuff with mushrooms when you know I prefer *meat*." He plopped his spoon into his half-empty bowl, causing splatter on the yellow tablecloth. Ronnie frowned, eyeing it. "Yet I still eat it."

"Edward...let's just finish eating, okay?" Ronnie finally said. She handed him a cloth napkin, her eyes still on his spill.

Edward eyed her for a moment before taking the napkin. "Yeah. Okay."

Once dinner was done and the kitchen was clean, Ronnie retreated upstairs and Edward parked it in the living room. He needed a break from her. Clicking the flatscreen TV onto ESPN, he just focused on what was on the screen, trying to erase the previous hour or so from his mind.

"Six years of this shit," he muttered to himself, rubbing his eyes.

He watched television until his eyes started to burn, then clicked it off. He could hear Ronnie moving around upstairs. Glancing above him, he sighed. Try as he might, he just couldn't seem to erase the tension that had taken root between them. And what was worse, it seemed like he was the only one trying.

When he entered their bedroom, Ronnie was kicking off her fuzzy slippers and tucking her long braids into a satin bonnet. Edward could smell the fruity scent of the body wash she just used in the shower. He eyed her smooth legs, automatically imagining them wrapped around his waist or draped over his shoulders.

Crossing the room, he took her into his arms and nuzzled her neck.

"What are you doing?" She gave a nervous chuckle.

"What do you think?" Grabbing the side of her face, he leaned down and kissed her, his other hand languidly sliding to her backside. She seemed to respond to him for a moment, but suddenly she was pushing him away. She eyed him apologetically.

"It's been four months, Ronnie," he reminded her, his voice gruff with various kinds of frustration.

"I know; I'm sorry. I'm just not in the mood tonight."

"You're never in the mood. Why can't you just indulge me?"

Her eyes widened slightly. "Indulge you? So I'm supposed to just lay there and let you have your way?"

"Hell, I'll take it. It's better than what I've been getting."

"Edward, I promise I'll make it up to you…"

"You do realize your I.O.U. list is a mile long, right?"

"I need your patience."

"What is it you think you've been getting? I've been nothing *but* patient. And I'm sick of having to jack off when my sexy wife is laying within arm's reach."

"It's *my* body, Edward. I don't really need a reason."

"I might buy that if we were just dating. But I'm your husband. And if you don't want to have sex with me, I deserve an actual reason."

"I just haven't been feeling very sexual, Edward. I don't expect you to understand."

"Well, *I'm* feeling sexual. But I guess that doesn't matter either, right?"

"Of course it does!"

"I sure can't tell. It's not like we were doing it that much before. Now we're not doing it at *all*?"

"Edward—"

"Forget it." Edward held up his hand. He rounded the bed and yanked back the covers. "Whatever excuse you're about to give me this time, keep it. It's not like it'll make any damn difference."

"Edward, please. Don't be mad..."

"Leave me alone."

He turned his back to her and cut off the bedside lamp, darkening his side of the room. Ronnie just stood on the other side of the bed, looking at him, wishing she could find the words to buy a little more time and understanding. Eventually, she just got into bed and turned off her own lamp, completing the darkness around them.

A couple of days later, Ronnie spent the day running errands. When she finally got home, the back of her Honda Pilot full of groceries, cleaning supplies and plastic bins, she sent Edward a text to ask him to come help bring everything into the house. She started bringing her purchases in through the garage, putting things away as she always did, humming her usual nameless tune. She was almost done with everything when she noticed Edward never came to help her.

Frowning curiously, Ronnie headed upstairs. His car was in the garage, so she knew Edward was home. It wasn't like him to not come help her after she went shopping; he should've been expecting her text.

"Edward?"

"In here."

Ronnie entered their bedroom. Edward was sitting on the bed, looking at her somberly.

"Edward, what are you..." It was then that she noticed the boxes. She could tell from where she was standing that half of the closet was empty. A sick feeling began sprouting from her gut.

"It's all your stuff," Edward confirmed, seeing her questioning look.

She looked at him, her chest heaving slightly. "What's going on, Edward?"

"I'm done. That's what's going on."

"What do you mean, *you're done*? Done with what?"

"You've got a fancy degree from Spelman. It's not hard to figure out. I'm leaving you."

"Wh-just like that? Why??"

"Because I'm not trying to live another day unhappy when I don't have to. And I've been unhappy for too long now."

Her hand flew to her chest. "Because of *me*?"

"Yes, because of *you*, Ronnie."

"Is this all because we haven't been having sex? Look, if you just give me a little more time—"

"It's not all about that." Edward stood, sliding his hands into his pockets. "You don't know how many nights I've laid in this bed agonizing over this. How many times I delayed coming home because I didn't want to eat one of your whack vegetarian meals or get the updated version of your 'honey-do' list. I don't work fifty hours a week just to spend my weekends cleaning the gutters."

"I'm sorry," Ronnie cried, rushing over to him. She gripped the front of his shirt, the tears running down her face. "I'll do better..."

"No, you won't." Edward shook his head sadly. "How many times have you said that already? I just don't believe you anymore, Ronnie."

"Edward! I love you! And I *know* you love me!"

"Yes, I do." His hands covered hers. "This is not something I want to do. I've put it off for weeks, trying to find any excuse not to. But I've been making every concession for you and you don't make *any* for me."

"That's not true!"

"Yes, it is. You know it is."

"Well, let's go to counseling! How can you just give up on us so easily? We've been married for six years!"

"Look at my face, Ronnie; this is anything *but* easy for me." Edward's own eyes were glistening with unshed tears. The pain of what he was doing along with seeing his wife's tears was tearing his heart apart. "And if I thought counseling would do any good, I'd make an appointment tomorrow. But if you won't tell *me* anything, why would I believe you'd tell a counselor?"

Ronnie looked at him pleadingly, the tears running in streams.

"This right here?" Edward glanced towards their hands. "This is the most affection we've had in weeks. Just how long do you honestly expect me to live like that, without any explanation as to why?"

Sniffling, Ronnie stepped back. "Have you met someone else? Is this about another woman?"

"No, I haven't. I haven't cheated on you, I haven't met anybody else, none of that. This is all about you and me, Ronnie. We don't even kiss or hug or cuddle, let alone have sex. You take better care of this house than you do of me. I-I just can't live another day like this." He squeezed her hands, touching his forehead to hers as his own tears started to run.

"Where am I supposed to go?" Ronnie whimpered. "Please, don't to this to us, Edward. Please..."

They stood there crying together until Edward suddenly dropped her hands and headed for the door. Right before leaving the room, he stopped.

"Whatever it is you have going on with you," he said, his back still turned. "Please get some help."

Ronnie just stood there crying, hoping he'd come back.

Chapter 1

Ronnie walked up to the familiar red door with the peeling paint. This was the last place she wanted to be, but she had no choice.

After several moments of hesitation, she finally knocked on the door. Wringing her hands, she looked anxiously around her, wondering if any of the same people still lived in the neighborhood and if they were watching her through their windows like they used to do back in the day.

Finally, the door swung open. An older man, gruff, grayed, and not looking thrilled to see her, stood there.

"Hey, Dad."

Pat Duncan just grunted. "Ya made it."

"Yeah."

"Well come on in here. Where's ya stuff?"

"My, um, my boxes are in the car." Ronnie jerked a thumb towards the Honda Pilot Edward so graciously let her keep.

"Guess I should help ya bring 'em in..."

"No, it's okay. I got it."

"Well, hurry up. I got dinner on the stove."

Ronnie could smell the fried meat already. Pressing a hand to her stomach, she quickly turned and hurried back to her car, wishing she could just get in and drive away.

After she lugged all of her boxes inside, she placed her hands on her hips and looked around. Everything looked the same since the day she moved out, when she left for college. Her eyes wandered to a gold-framed picture on the wooden bookcase of her mother, Missy. A few things around it were covered with a light film of dust, but the frame was shiny and clean. She lightly touched the frame wistfully.

Pat was in the kitchen. It sounded like he was talking to himself, but Ronnie couldn't make out what he was saying. She figured he was in there alone, because he never enjoyed having company.

With a shake of her head, she started transporting her boxes to her old bedroom. When she kicked open the door, she discovered that it had been redecorated. The formerly pale pink walls were now a dark royal blue; her frilly bedspread had been replaced with a navy and silver one. A dark wood desk now sat where her white vanity with the lighted mirror used to be.

"Wow," Ronnie marveled. "I bet he did this the day after I moved out."

Not believing all of this was happening, she started putting her things away. She only removed the things she knew she would need immediately from the boxes, as she hoped to high heaven she wouldn't be there all that long. She could tell already that this just wasn't going to work for very long.

"Come on and eat!" Pat yelled from the kitchen.

Ronnie started to yell back that she wasn't hungry, but changed her mind and headed towards the kitchen. Pat was piling his plate with fried pork chops, candied yams, and greens with bacon. Ronnie immediately felt queasy.

"I'll just have some lemon water," Ronnie declared. "I'm...not all that hungry."

"Suit yaself." Pat's back was still turned to her. "Lemons in the 'fridgerator."

Pat took his plate to the round wooden kitchen table as Ronnie went about fixing her drink. She joined him at the table and looked around the room, noting that it was pretty much exactly the same as she remembered.

"You've made some changes around here," she said after several moments of silence.

Pat picked up his pork chop and took a big bite with one hand, and shoved a forkful of greens into his mouth with the other. "Yep."

Ronnie's nose crinkled in disgust as she watched him devour his food. "You know, you really shouldn't be..."

He looked at her, his lips greasy as he chewed. His eyes were almost daring her.

"Shouldn't be eating so fast," Ronnie finally said, opting not to lecture him on the dangers of his beloved soul food. She hadn't even been there an hour yet. "Could lead to obesity, you know."

Pat waved a dismissive hand. "I ain't worried about that."

Biting her tongue, Ronnie decided to leave it at that for now.

She took a sip of her lemon water and glanced around the kitchen. It was cluttered and dusty, like the living room. Several old appliances were fighting for space on the aged laminate countertops. The stove was older than Ronnie. She remembered most of the magnets on the refrigerator from her childhood.

"Kitchen still looks the same," she finally commented.

"Umph."

"Living room, too."

"Uh-huh."

"Only place that I've seen so far that looks completely different is my old room."

Pat took a long gulp of his sweet tea and belched. "Yeah."

"Seems like all of my stuff is gone; there's not even any pictures of me displayed anywhere."

He finally looked at her. "So?"

"I can't help but wonder why that is."

Shrugging, Pat speared his last candied yam. "Figured you wouldn't be coming back. Ya ain't been back in years."

Neither has Mama, but all of her stuff is still up as if she were here this morning.

Ronnie kept that thought to herself as she took another sip of her lemon water, already wondering how long she was going to have to stay here.

There was no more forced conversation. After dinner, Pat cleaned up the kitchen, refusing Ronnie's offer to help. She noticed that there was quite a few leftovers, all of which Pat stuffed into plastic containers and stashed in the fridge. Ronnie started to ask why he made so much, but figured maybe he simply forgot her telling him that she was a vegetarian.

When the kitchen was clean, Pat kicked off his shoes and relaxed on the couch in the living room with a cold can of Bud Light, watching an old movie. Not wanting to subject either of them to more strained small talk, Ronnie wordlessly retreated to her room, sighing heavily as soon as she was behind the closed door.

"There is no way this is gonna work," she mumbled to herself. She hadn't even been there a day and she was already miserable. Pat didn't seem at all glad to see her, even though they hadn't seen or spoken to each other in years. When she went to college, Ronnie tried to forget this part of her life. It was almost embarrassing that she had to come crawling back because she had no place else to go.

She grabbed her cell phone and called Edward. Maybe if she pleaded her case and promised to make love to him every single night, he would reconsider and take her back. She would tell him whatever he wanted to hear, as long as it meant she didn't have to stay in this house with her dad.

The phone rang and rang. When she heard Edwards's voicemail, Ronnie hung up and tried again. This time, it went straight to voicemail. He was ignoring her calls already?

Undeterred, Ronnie sat up straighter, pushing some braids out of her face as she prepared to leave a message:

"Hey, Edward, sweetie. Look, I know you're still upset with me and you think I'm holding out on you, and I am so, so sorry. Please, if you just give me another chance, I promise I will be more cooperative, in *every* way. You can eat whatever you want, and I won't say a word about it. I won't bug you about doing anything to the house. I'll watch ESPN with you all day. Just please, call me back. Please?"

Ronnie hated how desperate she sounded, but she was in no position to be proud. She had no job, no training, a thousand dollars in the bank (another consolation gift from Edward), and no friends to speak of. And her Sociology degree wasn't exactly a golden ticket to big bucks.

When her phone didn't ring in the next ten minutes, Ronnie tossed it onto the bed. The emotions were swirling in her chest. Edward wouldn't even talk to her. They were college sweethearts, and he threw their relationship away just because things were a little rough. Ronnie was angry, but mostly, she was sad.

Glancing around the room, she wandered over to the desk, pulling the drawer open with two fingers. She was surprised to see a photo album in there. Picking it up, she ran a hand over the faded gold lettering on the white leather cover, remembering when the album was practically new. Her mind raced back to the day she and Missy bought it from the K-Mart across town, then came home and filled it up with pictures.

"This is gonna be your special album, baby," Missy had told her. Ronnie was about ten years old then; they were sitting next to each other on the couch with Ronnie nestled under Missy's arm, which was her favorite spot. "All of our memories of you are gonna go right in here."

It was the only album with Ronnie's pictures; she recalled that all of the other albums were filled with pictures of her parents or other family members. Ronnie used to think she was special for getting an album all to herself; she used to look through it all the time. Yet when she left for Spelman, she didn't even consider taking it with her. She didn't want any reminders.

With a hitched breath, she sat on the bed and opened the album. There was her original birth certificate...a picture of Missy holding her shortly after giving birth, with Pat standing near the bed. The smile on his face was strained, while Missy's was glowing. There were pictures of her in diapers, of Missy playing with her on the floor, of her in a poufy pink Easter dress, her first day of kindergarten. All kinds of milestones, professional pictures and casual ones, and plenty of shots of her and Missy doing regular things like baking a pie, folding laundry or making crafts at the kitchen table. It was the last time Ronnie could remember being genuinely happy.

When she got to one of the last pictures in the album, the tears welled up all on their own. It was one of the few pictures of the three of them. Ronnie remembered the day like it was yesterday; Missy and Pat had argued that morning, because Pat hadn't wanted to go get the pictures taken. Ronnie could hear them through the closed bedroom door. Missy had been speaking in hushed tones while Pat didn't seem to care if Ronnie heard them or not. Pat ultimately relented, but he didn't try to act happy about it.

Ronnie peered at the photo. One barely-there smile. One forced, resolved smile. And one guilty one. Ronnie was the one that had asked if they could go down to Sears as a family and get the picture taken. Missy had been all for it but Pat? Not so much.

Slamming the album closed and shoving it to the floor, Ronnie climbed under the covers fully clothed and cried herself to sleep.

Chapter 2

The strong smell of bacon make Ronnie's nose itch.

It was barely five o'clock the next morning and Pat was already up making breakfast. He always had been an early riser, thanks to years of early start times at the shutter factory. Even in his retirement, his morning routine pretty much stayed the same.

Ronnie buried her face in the pillow and tried to go back to sleep, but it was futile. She couldn't ignore that stench. With a groan, she threw the covers back and scratched her head, immediately regretting not putting on her satin bonnet before laying down the previous night. She had been too emotional to even think about that.

She plucked some clothes and toiletries from one of her boxes and went to take a shower. By the time she finished, Pat was almost done with his breakfast.

"Good morning," she greeted pleasantly.

"Mornin.'"

Ronnie looked at the stove and saw the fried eggs, bacon, and raisin toast, and knew she would need to go to the grocery store. She had already seen he had practically nothing in the refrigerator that she could make a meal out of; it was like he didn't believe in vegetables. There were just a few sweet potatoes on the counter and one lone yellow apple, which was her least favorite kind.

"Do you mind if I have one of these sweet potatoes?" she asked.

"Help yaself."

She grabbed the biggest one, pricked it all over with a fork, then stuck it in the oven.

"And the apple?"

"Knock yaself out."

Ronnie rinsed the fruit off and cut it into slices before putting it on a chipped saucer and joining Pat at the table. He was reading yesterday's paper and munching on yet another slice of bacon, seemingly having no interest in conversation. Ronnie checked her phone, disappointed to see no messages from Edward.

After a while of playing on her word search app, Ronnie put her phone down. "How come you cook so much? It looks like you have enough for at least three people over there."

Pat shrugged.

"You know all that pork is bad for you."

Pat didn't even look up. "Folks say some'a everything is bad for ya nowadays."

"It is, though. It's full of saturated fat, not to mention all the sodium—"

"I don't need no nutrition lesson," Pat snapped, slapping his paper down on the table. "I said you could stay here but I don't need you houndin' me 'bout what I eat."

Slightly taken aback, Ronnie stated, "I'm just trying to help you, Dad. And *speaking* of me staying here, did you forget me telling you I was a vegetarian?"

"Naw, I ain't forget."

Ronnie frowned. "But there's almost no vegetables in the refrigerator."

"You bein' a vegetarian is yo' business. I'm gon' buy what I always buy."

"Still stubborn as ever, I see," Ronnie muttered, biting into an apple slice.

"Don't think you can talk back to me!" Pat warned, raising the folded newspaper as if he was gonna smack her with it. "You still the child, I don't care how old you get!"

Not putting it past him to whack her with that newspaper, Ronnie stopped talking. It was just another indication that she needed to come up with a plan to get out of there, and quickly, because there was no way this was going to work.

• • • •

LATER THAT DAY, RONNIE went to the nearby Walmart for some groceries and cleaning supplies, ignoring the strong sense of déjà vu. Knowing she had limited funds, she was mindful of every penny she spent, already missing her expanded budget when she and Edward were together.

She wandered up and down the aisles with her notepad and calculator, feeling humiliated even though no one was paying her any attention. It was like the stench of being separated, jobless and living with her father was radiating to everyone around her. Ronnie just wanted to rewind the clock to a week or so before and make all new decisions. Maybe then she wouldn't be in this mess.

"Ronnie Duncan?"

Turning around, Ronnie recognized her old high school classmate, Tess Bryant. Just as noticeable as ever, Tess drew attention with her booming voice, brightly colored outfits and large, fluffy afro. The fact that she was almost six feet tall didn't hurt, either.

"Tess," Ronnie smiled, hoping it looked sincere. She had hoped not to run into anyone she knew. "My surname is actually Blake now. How are you? I haven't seen you in years."

"Yep, not since our five-year reunion. You weren't at the ten-year one, right?"

"No, I missed that. What's been going on with you?"

"Oh girl, I got my own hair salon across town. Got tired of working for other folks. We've been open for about three years now."

"Oh wow; that's awesome. Congratulations." *Please don't ask me what I do...*

"So what do you do?"

"I'm actually taking some time off to spend with my father," Ronnie said, her voice even. She hated to lie, but there was no way she was going to divulge her real situation. "He's not doing so well, you know."

"Oh damn, I'm sorry to hear that," Tess replied sincerely. "You said your last name is Blake now? How long have you been married?" She eyed the one carat diamond that Ronnie still wore.

"Six years. What about you?" Ronnie quickly detracted. "Did you and that football player ever get married? What was his name...Marques?"

"Oh yeah, girl, that was him. But nope; we broke up not too long after graduation. He wasn't trying to have a long distance thing going and I wasn't, either. He went off to Missouri on that scholarship and I haven't seen him since."

"I'm sorry."

Tess waved a hand, her large multicolored rings glistening in the light. "No need to be. It was a high school relationship; we never planned on getting married or anything, anyway."

"Oh." Ronnie glanced at her watch, even though there was absolutely no need for her to rush. It wasn't like she had anywhere to be. "Well it was so good to see you again, Tess. You're looking great."

"Thank you, girl! So are you!" Tess pulled out a business card from her large green purse and handed it to her. "Don't be a stranger. Are you on Facebook or Instagram?"

"Oh, uh no...I never really got into social media."

"Oh okay. Well definitely keep my card, then. If you want to chat or even come get your hair done or something, though your braids are tight, girl."

"Thank you." Ronnie ran a hand through the microbraids that she knew she wouldn't be able to afford getting again anytime soon. She started to ask if Tess would give her some kind of discount, but thought better of it. She didn't want to offend Tess by asking for a favor when they hadn't seen each other in years, and it's not like they had been best friends in high school. And if Tess was anything like she was back then, Ronnie didn't put it past her to go off on her if she took offense to the request.

"Well, it was great seeing you, Tess."

"You too!"

Ronnie tucked Tess's card into her pocket and pushed her cart away. She marveled at the fact that Tess had her own business; back in the day, all she cared about was partying and hugging up on her boyfriend, not taking a lot of things all that seriously. Ronnie had been the opposite, focusing on her studies and piling up extracurricular activities that would look good on her college applications. Purely fun social activities were few and far between. But a lot of good all that did her now. She had nothing while Tess was apparently thriving in business for herself.

When she got back to Pat's, she shook her head when she noticed that he had forgotten to lock the door. Making a mental note to say something to him about that, she took her bags into the kitchen and sat them on the table. When she opened the refrigerator, though, she frowned. There was almost no room for her things, as Pat had it filled with packs of meat, containers of leftovers, beer and jugs of juice and milk, and other things. It seemed fuller than it had that morning. Ronnie looked at her bags of fresh produce and wondered how in the world she was going to squeeze it in amongst all of Pat's things. Really, she didn't even want her fruits and veggies on the same shelves with Pat's heart-clogging meats, but she had nowhere else to put it.

After several minutes of maneuvering, Ronnie managed to get all of her things into the refrigerator. She put her non-perishables into the pantry before taking her new cleaning supplies to her room. After changing into a tank and some leggings, she began cleaning the house, starting in her room. Humming to herself, she dusted, scrubbed, and polished, remembering all of the tips and tricks Missy taught her when they would clean the house together on Saturday mornings.

When Pat came in, he wasn't too happy about her taking such initiative.

"Who told you to do this?" he demanded, his frown deep.

Ronnie, confused by his anger, turned off the vacuum. "What do you mean? Nobody *told* me to. I'm just trying to help."

"No ya ain't. You tryin' to come in here and take over."

Frowning, Ronnie placed a hand on her hip. "Take over what? I just saw it needed to be done, so I volunteered to clean up. I would think you'd be a little more appreciative."

"Appreciative? I can clean my own house, thank you!"

"I just noticed things were a little dusty and figured you didn't have the energy or something. I don't see what the big deal is."

Pat grunted. "Ya shoulda asked first."

"Asked? To clean up? What if I came in here and left a mess in my wake? Then you'd probably be fussing about *that*. I never *could* win with you!"

"This ain't about winning nothin'. Maybe I liked stuff the way it was."

"Why would you *like* living around a bunch of dust? Not only does it look bad, it's not healthy. The more you breathe that stuff in—"

"You just an expert on everything, ain't ya? I told you, don't come in here lecturin' me about every little thing."

Stopping her retort, Ronnie held up her hands and took a breath, trying to calm herself. "Dad, I am not trying to lecture you. You clearly don't know, so I'm simply informing you, that's all."

"You always *did* think you knew more than everybody else. Don't nobody like a know-it-all."

"I'm not a—"

"You always naggin' and thinkin' you know every damn thing is probably the reason yo' mama left here," Pat snarled. "I always said you thought you was better than everybody, especially us."

Any thoughts of keeping the peace were now out the window. Anger spread over Ronnie's body like a rash at lightning speed.

"*Maybe* the reason she left is because you're so stubborn and negative, never having anything positive to say about anything," Ronnie countered, her frown now matching her father's. "Nothing is ever good enough for you!"

"Hmph. I don't know how you would know, no way. Ain't stepped foot in this house since the day you went off to college, and hardly ever called. Even before that, you had that calendar on the wall countin' down the days 'til you could leave here. You think yo' mama didn't see that? Think that didn't hurt her feelin's?"

"Dad, I was only *fifteen* when she left! Mama and I always got along great, and she knew how much I was looking forward to college. *Your* negativity has been going on as long as I can remember! I don't know how she lived with it as long as she did!"

Looking like he was about to explode, Pat stormed to his bedroom and slammed the door so hard, the walls shook. Ronnie jumped, then sighed, running her hands over her face. Her heart was racing. It was the first time she and Pat had directly addressed Missy leaving to each other. Truth was, they didn't know why Missy left; one day when Ronnie got home from debate club practice and Pat got home from work, Missy was gone. Ronnie always thought Pat's eternal sour attitude had finally driven her away. Apparently, Pat had been blaming Ronnie all of these years, too.

Exhausted, Ronnie flopped onto the couch and looked at the old light blue carpet that was well past its prime. Ronnie could remember when it was brand new. She looked at the big box TV set and recalled the day Pat had brought it home, announcing that when he was home, no one was to bother it. The coffee table where Pat often propped his feet without taking his shoes off. Missy never did like that, from what Ronnie remembered.

Not wanting to conjure up any more unpleasant memories, Ronnie shook her head and shot up off the couch. She wasn't quite done vacuuming, but she yanked the cord from the wall and wrapped it up. She didn't want to give Pat reason to come back out there starting round two of accusations and arguments. Especially since she had a feeling that their next disagreement would most likely be coming sooner rather than later, as it was.

She quietly finished her cleaning, and thankfully by the time Pat emerged from his room, she was done. When he stomped into the living room, he paused and looked around, sniffing the air. Ronnie, who was on the couch perusing jobs on her laptop, didn't acknowledge him. When Pat saw that the unfamiliar linen fresh scent was courtesy of the plug-in near the television, he just grunted and continued to the kitchen. Ronnie had purchased a few of them earlier that day to freshen up the stale air, not to mention help eliminate the ever-present odor of Pat's unhealthy meals. If she had to stay there, Ronnie at least wanted to be somewhat comfortable. And constantly smelling old grease in the air didn't help that effort.

When she heard the clanging of pans, she figured Pat was about to start making dinner. Scooping up her laptop, Ronnie retreated to her room and closed the door. She was in the living room because the Wi-Fi was stronger there, but she would rather endure spotty connection than smell whatever fattening meal Pat was about to make.

"Come on and eat!"

Ronnie scowled. Surely Pat didn't think she was going to eat whatever he made, whatever it was. She was surprised he was even speaking to her after the argument they had.

Nevertheless, she closed her laptop and hesitantly trudged to the kitchen. She perused the stovetop laden with fried chicken legs, macaroni and cheese, and blackeyed peas. Her nose instantly crinkled in disgust but she straightened her expression before Pat saw it.

"Um, I'm just gonna make myself a salad," she informed him, inching towards the refrigerator.

Pat didn't look at her as he poured himself a big cup of sweet tea. "I figured."

"Oh. I just figured since you made so much again, plus you called me in here to eat..."

"It's dinnertime. Plus, I'm 'bout to have some company."

"Who?" Ronnie instinctively asked.

As if on cue, there was a knock on the door. Pat wordlessly went to answer it. When he reentered the kitchen, Ronnie frowned when she saw who was following him.

"Ronnie!" Her uncle Alvin exclaimed, rushing over to her. He pulled her into a hearty hug, squeezing her tightly, seemingly oblivious to her displeasure. Ronnie wanted to elude him but her feet seemed to be stuck where they were. "It is so good to see you! It's been too long!"

Ronnie eased away from her uncle's embrace. "Uncle Alvin."

"How have you been? I was so glad to hear it when Pat mentioned you were gonna be staying here with him for a while. Family should be together."

Ronnie wanted to be anywhere else but there. "I've been okay. Dad didn't mention you were coming."

"Oh yeah, we're just gonna eat and play some cards. You wanna join us?"

"Actually, I have to run; I just remembered something I need to take care of." Ronnie was already turning towards the door.

"Oh no," Alvin looked disappointed. "I was hoping we could get caught up. It's been years since I've seen my favorite niece."

"Sorry." Not wanting to say anything else, she quickly turned and rushed to her bedroom.

"Don't mind her," she heard Pat tell his brother. "She always been dramatic."

Ignoring this, Ronnie slipped on her shoes and grabbed her keys and purse. Hurrying out of the back door so she wouldn't have to pass by Pat or her uncle, Ronnie hustled to her car and drove off, not even knowing where she was going.

After about a half hour of mindlessly driving around, Ronnie ended up at LA Fitness. Pulling into the parking lot, she took a deep breath and tried to shake off her lingering anxiety.

"Yeah, a good workout will do me some good," she said to herself. Her fingers rapidly tapped the steering wheel. "I need to burn off some of this...frustration."

She grabbed her duffel bag that she kept in the back of her car and headed inside. But her slowly brightening spirits were soon doused again.

"What do you mean my membership has been cancelled??" she exclaimed.

"I'm sorry, Ronnie, but Edward came in and did it yesterday," the receptionist informed her regretfully.

Flustered, Ronnie glanced around her before leaning forward and lowering her voice, suddenly mindful of everyone hearing her predicament. "Deena, come on; you *know* me. I've been coming here for years!"

"Yeah, I do know you, and if it were up to me I'd tell you to go on in, but it's not." Deena held up her hands helplessly. "Why don't you just start your own membership?"

Ronnie felt her face flush. There was no way she was about to admit that she couldn't afford a membership there on her own. The thought that Edward would be so petty as to cancel her gym membership of all things fired up her insides like a wood oven.

"I'll have to come back and do that another day," she muttered before turning to leave.

"Ronnie, wait."

She turned around hopefully.

"I'll need your membership card back."

Her face flaming, Ronnie slapped her card on the raised desk and hurried out, keeping her eyes averted from anyone. She was sure the people that had been waiting behind her heard that entire conversation. Whenever she *was* able to afford to renew her membership, she already knew she would have to find another gym. She would be too embarrassed to come back in here after this.

She headed straight for Edward's. This was getting ridiculous. If she could just talk to him face to face, she was certain that they could reach some kind of understanding. Him being angry at her didn't mean he had to cut her off at the knees simply because he could.

Using her key, she entered the house and looked around. It felt like she hadn't been there in months, and it had only been a few days. She started to head upstairs when she heard Edward's voice in the kitchen.

Taking a deep breath, she ran through what she was going to say in her head as she started towards him, but when she heard another voice, a woman's voice, she stopped in her tracks.

"This is *so* good, Eddie."

Eddie?

"It *is* good, huh?" Edward replied. "You have no idea how much I've been missing this."

With that, Ronnie stormed into the kitchen, bracing herself for some kind of illicit countertop scene. But what she saw was her husband and some other woman standing near the stove eating bacon-wrapped scallops from a take-out container. They both looked at Ronnie when she rushed into the room, startled.

"Ronnie, what are you doing here?" Edward asked, his surprise quickly giving way to annoyance.

"I needed to talk to you and I knew you wouldn't answer your phone." Ronnie eyed the other woman, getting the strange feeling she'd seen her before.

"I'll leave you two alone," the woman offered, starting to leave.

Edward placed a hand on her arm, stopping her. Ronnie's breath hitched at the simple action.

"Stay here; I'll be right back," Edward told her. He walked over to Ronnie, his eyes clearly not pleased. "Come on."

Ronnie didn't move. "Aren't you gonna introduce me, Edward?" She was still eyeing the woman. *I could probably take her, if I had to.*

"I wasn't planning on it but fine. Ronnie, this is Nivea. Nivea, Ronnie."

"It's nice to meet you, Ronnie," Nivea smiled pleasantly. "It's so nice to finally put a face with the name."

"Excuse me?" Ronnie frowned, confused. Did Edward discuss her with his mistress? Did they lay around in bed and talk about what a crappy wife Ronnie had been?

Before Nivea could speak again, Edward took Ronnie's arm and started leading her out of the kitchen, asking Nivea to give him a minute, and to not eat the rest of the scallops. Ronnie was dismayed by their comfortable rapport; just how long had they been sleeping together?

And if Edward had Nivea, why was he always on her back about sex?

"You seem as if you're in a hurry to get rid of me," she said once they were in the living room. "This is going to take longer than a 'minute,' Edward."

"No, it isn't, because as you can see, I'm busy. And I really don't appreciate you coming over here unannounced."

"Well, maybe if you would answer your damn phone..."

Edward sighed, rubbing his temples. It seemed like Ronnie was the last person he wanted to deal with. "What is it, Ronnie?"

"I just came from the gym. I can't believe you cancelled my membership. Do you have any idea how humiliating that was? You could've at least given me a heads-up."

"Ronnie, believe it or not, I'm not trying to be cruel. But I told you when we decided to separate-"

"*We* didn't decide to separate. *You* decided and just dragged me along with you. And I guess I see why now." Ronnie swept an arm in the direction of the kitchen. "You sure didn't waste any time, huh?"

"What are you talking about?"

"I'm talking about you already having another woman in here not even a week after putting me out. How long have you been sleeping with her, Edward?"

His frown melted with realization. "You think Nivea is my mistress or something?"

"Well, you've got her up in our kitchen in the evening, in a clingy dress and heels like it's some kind of date..."

"I told you I never cheated on you and I meant it. Nivea is my sister-in-law. You might know that if you had gone with me to any of my family reunions like I asked you to. Or to my brother's wedding that you bailed on at the last minute because you suddenly didn't feel well. Remember that?"

Feeling silly but trying not to show it, Ronnie stood her ground. "Okay, I stand corrected on that, but what about the gym membership? Why are you trying to leave me with nothing?"

"Like I was trying to say, this isn't about me trying to be cruel. But if we're gonna make a clean break, I need to cut all ties to you. And that includes any accounts that you have in my name. I don't want you using that stuff as an excuse to stay in contact with me."

"Wow. This is you not trying to be cruel?"

"That came out a little worse than I meant it to, but it's true. The Pilot is paid for; I let you keep that. I gave you some money. You're staying with your Pops, so that should tide you over for a while. And I'll be as fair as I can in the settlement."

Ronnie looked up at him. "Settlement?"

"The divorce settlement."

It wasn't a total surprise, but Ronnie still hadn't expected the D-word so soon. She couldn't help the stinging tears. "Was I that horrible that you want to get rid of me so quickly?"

Edward sighed again. He moved like he was about to put his arms around her, but stopped himself, sliding his hands into his pockets. "No, you weren't horrible. But like I said, I was unhappy and had been for a long while. Despite that, though, Ronnie, I still love you. And I don't want to give myself time to talk myself out of what I know I need to do."

Ronnie started to plead and try to convince him that he *didn't* need to do this; that they could give their marriage another try. But she couldn't bring herself to beg him again. She'd done that several times over the phone and her cries went ignored.

"I see," she finally said, her eyes on the ground. "And let me guess; the papers are already drawn up, huh?"

Edward nodded, averting his own eyes. He didn't look any happier about this situation than Ronnie did.

"Should I sign them now? Don't wanna delay you getting on with your life," Ronnie said in a clipped tone. Her skin was shaking with the realization that her marriage was actually over, and that there was nothing she could do about it.

Edward's eyes pleaded with her. "Let's make this as amicable as possible, Ronnie."

"Right, because I wouldn't want to get blamed for that, too. You might take the shoes off my feet or something. After all, you bought them."

Shaking his head, Edward chose to ignore Ronnie's sarcasm. "The papers can be signed in the next couple of days. I'll let you know. And...just so you know, I'll also be changing the locks."

"Of course you will. Because you don't want my prudish, uncommunicative, veggie-loving ass up in your house. I totally understand." She took the house keys from her keychain and dropped them on a nearby end table. "There. You happy?"

"I'm not happy about any of this, Ronnie."

"Well, you're doing a masterful job of hiding that."

"You can't say that I didn't try to save our marriage. I expressed my concerns, tried to talk, tried to suggest ways to shake things up and you weren't trying to hear any of it. Not saying I was perfect, but *I* tried."

"And I didn't?"

"No, I really don't think you did, Ronnie, which was the problem. You didn't take my concerns seriously. You treated me like some ungrateful child that didn't know what was best for himself. I'm thirty-six years old; I didn't need another mother. I needed a *wife*." He looked at her with a shrug of his shoulders. "And you couldn't be that to me."

Ronnie tried hard to maintain her composure, but with every second she looked at Edward, the handsome chocolate man she had loved since she was a nineteen-year-old college sophomore, she knew she was going to break. A larger part than she realized had been holding out hope that she and Edward could somehow salvage things; that maybe he would miss her so much that he would be willing to overlook her supposed faults. But apparently not.

Taking in a slow sweep of him, from his low-cut black hair to the loafers on his size-twelve feet, Ronnie quickly swiped at her fat tears and took what was meant to be a resolving breath.

"I'm sorry." Her voice was even. "I'm sorry I couldn't be what you needed."

She left, quietly closing the door to her safety net behind her.

Chapter 3

As he did every night, Pat went about making dinner, pulling out all of the ingredients.

"Didn't we say we were gonna have some fried green tomatoes soon?" he muttered, peering into the refrigerator. "I'm outta cornmeal, though. I'll have to make 'em next week, after I go to the store."

Dropping a couple of eggs into a big bowl of ground beef, sautéed onions, peppers and various seasonings, Pat continued to mutter to himself.

"Gotta get the brakes on the car looked at. Heard some squeakin'." He hummed a nameless tune as he stirred the recipe for Missy's favorite meatloaf. "That's the kinda stuff you gotta nip in the bud."

He continued to cook and talk, as he did every night. Ronnie was out, so he finished his meal of meatloaf, rice and peas in peace as he liked, recalling that morning's news stories. He got the bad ones out of the way first, putting as soft a spin on them as he could.

"You always said the news was too depressin'," he mentioned with a slight chuckle. "Never did like watchin' it, from the first day I met ya. But that's what I'm here for."

When he was done eating, he cleaned up the kitchen, stuffing the leftovers into the refrigerator. After showering, he laid out his clothes for church the next day. His routine had been the same for the past thirty years. He didn't want change.

He ironed his white button-down shirt and gray slacks, then went about choosing Missy's outfit. He decided on a long baby blue dress and laid it next to his clothes.

"Told ya I'd pick your favorite color next time," he said with a small satisfied smile. "Had to get it washed first. You know good and well you ain't gon' put on nothin' dirty, 'specially for church."

Kneeling beside his bed, he prayed for the good times to come back, then pulled his wedding album from underneath Missy's pillow. He settled his back against the wooden headboard as he slowly flipped through every page, marveling at the images as if it was his first time seeing them. Warmth spread over him. His wife was always the prettiest thing walking to him. Her honey brown eyes always gave away whatever she was feeling, even when she didn't want them to. Pat used to tease her that her lips might be able to lie, but her eyes never could.

When he got to their wedding picture, a somewhat grainy black-and-white shot taken in front of their tiny church, the tears came automatically, as they always did. He quickly glanced at his bedroom door to ensure it was closed before focusing again on the picture. Missy had gotten her chin-length hair curled special that day, in spirals. She let her mama talk her into putting on some makeup, though Pat never thought she needed it. What looked plain to most was refreshing to him. He knew exactly what he was getting.

He slammed the album shut suddenly, the memories becoming too much for him. Wiping his eyes, he moved the album to the other side of the bed and turned off the bedside lamp. Then, as he did every night, he pulled Missy's pillow that was wrapped in the last nightgown she wore before she left closer to him and drifted off to sleep.

The next morning, he got up at five to get breakfast started. His body felt heavy, but he ignored it. Not terribly hungry, he made an egg and sausage sandwich on toast, slathered with butter and grape jelly. He tried not to think about all of the baseball games that were going to be played that day; the Braves were playing the Mets in a doubleheader. He'd love nothing more than to kick back with some beer and pork rinds and just enjoy that, but Missy never liked for him to skip church.

When he finished eating, he went to get dressed. By the time he emerged, Ronnie was up, doing yoga in the living room. Pat realized he had temporarily forgotten about her.

"Good morning," she greeted pleasantly.

Pat noticed how she had pushed the coffee table off to the side, against the wooden bookcase. When he saw Missy's gold-framed picture knocked over, his temper flared.

"You see what you did!" he accused loudly, hurrying over to right the picture. "Why don't you watch what you doin'!"

Ronnie hadn't even realized she accidently knocked the picture over. "I'm sorry; I didn't notice-"

"Well, ya *shoulda* noticed." Pat carefully brushed off the dustless frame with his fingers before putting it back in its correct position. "Who told you you could come in here movin' stuff around?"

"I was just..." Ronnie sighed. Deciding it wasn't worth arguing about, she conceded. "I apologize; I didn't realize I knocked over the picture. I'll be more careful next time."

Pat glared at her. "Good." He retrieved his worn Bible from the shelf.

"You're leaving for church now?"

"Uh-huh." He paused. "Why ya askin'?"

"I made you breakfast."

Pat hadn't expected that. He glanced towards the kitchen then at Ronnie, whose honey brown eyes relayed she just wanted to keep the peace. It was probably the first time he looked right into her eyes in years, and he remembered part of the reason why he'd stopped. She looked too much like Missy.

Turning his head away, he grunted. "I ate already."

"Oh." Pat wasn't looking at her, but he could hear the disappointment in her voice.

He started for the door, his feet seeming to slow all on their own. Opening the door, he muttered, "But thank ya." Then he left.

Having heard him, Ronnie took a relieved breath. Her olive branch had remained mostly intact.

Pat sat in the fifth row on the right side, closest to the wall. He clapped along with the choir, murmured along with the prayers, and rocked side to side at the pastor's rousing words, his eyes closed. He never did say much during service. He just took everything in, giving long grunts of concurrence along with the occasional 'Amen.'

Ronnie hadn't been to church since she was a teenager, since Pat assumed she didn't start attending anywhere else after she left for college. Her home church wasn't so far from the Spelman campus that she couldn't still attend on Sundays, but she apparently chose not to. She didn't want anything to do with any of them; she made that clear when she left and never looked back until she had no choice but to do so.

When she was little, Ronnie used to squirm all through church service like she had ants in her pants. Missy always had more patience with her than Pat did. He wanted to take her out back and whip her legs with a switch, but Missy had the magic touch. She would just whisper something into Ronnie's ear, and whatever she said was enough to keep her still until service was over. Pat never asked what she would tell her, because he was too busy stewing that she had to say anything at all.

When the service was over, Pat stood and looked around the sanctuary, hoping to see that familiar face. His fingers anxiously tapped the back of the pew in front of him. He let out a relieved breath when he saw her approach him.

"Pat, it's so good to see you," Debra, his sister-in-law, greeted him with open arms.

"You, too." He gave her a quick embrace, then stepped back. "You been doin' all right?"

"Oh, I'm super blessed. You?"

He shrugged. "Can't complain, I reckon. I was wonderin' if you were gonna see me over here."

"It's hard to miss you. Especially since you sit in the same seat every Sunday."

"Force a' habit." He looked at her expectantly, signaling his fill of small talk. He wanted to know if she had anything for him today.

Recognizing the look, Debra reached into her purse and pulled out a postcard. She handed it to him with a small smile, glad that she would be able to give him what he needed.

Pat released a shaky breath as he took the postcard, the relief almost strong enough to knock him back on his heels. Every Sunday he looked for Debra like Santa Claus on Christmas morning, and that postcard was the only gift he wanted. There was never a return address and it only had a few words on it, but that didn't matter.

He ran his fingers over Missy's familiar handwriting.

"When did it come in?" he asked, voice low. His eyes were fixated.

"Just yesterday morning. I was so glad that you came today so I could give it to you. We at least know she's still okay, wherever she is."

Pat fought to maintain his composure. "I 'preciate it."

"I'm still praying that she'll come back. But at least she's keeping us posted that she's alive."

"I don't know why she sends these to you and not me."

Debra shook her head. "None of this makes any sense, Pat. We don't even know why she left in the first place."

He cleared his throat. "Yeah."

There were a few silent moments before Debra finally leaned over and give him another hug. She was used to this reaction.

"Love you, brother." She gave him a final squeeze on his arm before walking away.

Several more moments passed before Pat snapped out of it, looking around him as he tucked the postcard into his pocket. It had been a couple of months since the last one, and with every day that passed, he got more and more anxious. He could breathe easy, at least for now. He could keep up hope that his wife might still come back.

Chapter 4

The tension was too much.

Ronnie knew that she needed to hurry up and get a job. The sooner she saved some money, the sooner she could get her own place. She and Pat might as well have been two strangers, the way they treated each other. She tried to be the bigger person and make him some breakfast last Sunday morning, but he didn't want it. Even though he thanked her, Ronnie hadn't felt inclined to make that or any similar gesture since.

As far as Ronnie was concerned, Pat was a stubborn old goat and he was going to stay a stubborn old goat. He was just too set in his ways to change.

And, Ronnie felt a little betrayed that Pat was still letting her Uncle Alvin come around. Even if he didn't acknowledge it, he should've known that Ronnie didn't like him and hadn't for years. But apparently, that didn't matter, either.

Even though her funds were limited, Ronnie went out to do a little retail therapy at Ross. Buying a nice new dress would boost her spirits and her confidence, both of which she would need to go out and find a new job despite having no experience in anything.

She was perusing the stuffed racks, taking her time. Knowing she was only allowing herself one dress, she wanted to be sure she found just the right one. Even though she had plenty of clothes, there was nothing like a new dress for a new experience.

"Wow, twice in a little more than a week?"

Ronnie turned around, her automatic tight smile already in place. "Hey, Tess."

"Taking advantage of these bargains too, huh?"

"Oh yeah, absolutely."

"I feel you. I always find a bunch of cute stuff up in here. And there's always plenty of stuff that accommodates this voluptuousness."

Ronnie chuckled despite herself. Tess always had been proud of her curves. Ronnie was always curious of what bra size she wore but there was no way she was going to ask her that.

"There's definitely something for everybody. Hopefully they'll have the right thing for me to wear to a job interview."

"Oh, you're looking for a job? Where?"

"Not sure yet. I'm still...weighing some options." Ronnie cleared her throat.

"Well, if you don't mind working for an old classmate, you can come work in my shop,"

Tess offered. "I had to fire my last receptionist and I need someone to replace her."

"Oh!" Ronnie was clearly caught off guard. While she did need a job, the idea of sitting in a loud salon where people gossiped and cackled all day, not to mention inhaling the smell of chemicals and irons that either straightened, colored, or just burned the hair, did not appeal to her. "Oh, wow, Tess, that's so cool of you to ask. I don't know, though..."

"Come on, you'd be doing me a favor. I wouldn't have to go through the mind-numbing process of holding interviews and picking the cracked nuts from the bowl. And I'd much rather get somebody in there that I already know and trust."

Trust? "But...well, I have to tell you that I've never been a receptionist before..."

"Girl, it's answering the phone, setting appointments and getting beverages. It's not hard to learn."

"True. But—"

"Do you have some interviews line up already?"

"Well, no..."

"Have you even applied anywhere yet?"

"No."

"So I don't understand the hesitation. You need a job and I need to hire someone. And I *know* it's not that you think you're too good to work in a beauty salon. You're not stuck up like that."

Ronnie's face flushed slightly. "Of course not."

"I know being a receptionist isn't the dream, but it's at least something you can do to get you back on your feet."

Her eyes snapped to Tess. "What makes you think I'm...*off* my feet?"

Tess gave her a *who-do-you-think-you're-fooling?* look. "Let's just say I'm good at reading vibes."

Questions sprouted from Ronnie's brain like weeds in a garden. Exactly what vibe was it that Tess was getting from her?

"Not to mention, I have some really cool employees," Tess continued. "You can meet some new people, maybe make a new friend or two, if you want. But even if you don't, you'll be bringing home some bacon."

Feeling that it would be silly to amend Tess's statement to where she would be bringing home the *veggie* bacon, Ronnie finally conceded. She didn't even know why she was really hesitating in the first place.

"You're right, Tess. I appreciate you helping me out like this. When would you need me to start?"

"Why don't you come by on Wednesday? That way I can run you through everything and introduce you to the staff before the weekend, and you can just jump right in."

"That sounds good. I can do that."

"Nice! This is gonna be so lit, I know already! One thing to cross of my damn list; thank you, girl! You still got my card, right?"

"Oh, uh, yeah. Yeah, I still have it."

"The address and everything is on there. Come by around ten."

"I'll be there. Should I wear anything in particular?"

"You can wear jeans, as long as they're nice. We're not very formal. I'll have a shirt for you when you get there."

"Sounds good. Thanks so much, Tess."

"Thank *you*! Make sure you call me if you have any questions or anything."

After Tess sauntered off, Ronnie marveled at this latest development. She had come to Ross for a dress to wear to an interview and she came out with a job she didn't even have to apply for. She realized she hadn't asked how much she would be making, but it didn't matter. Whatever it was would be more than she was getting now. Finally, a little bit of good fortune.

She headed for the jeans section.

When Ronnie got back to Pat's a couple of hours later, Pat was in the living room, watching baseball. His feet were up on the coffee table, shoes on, and a cold beer was in his rough hand. He didn't even look up when she came in.

Ronnie started to stroll right by him without speaking but made herself stop walking. She looked at him for several moments, but he never acknowledged her.

She sighed. "I got a job today."

Pat grunted.

"Just thought I'd let you know."

He took a sip of his beer. "'Kay."

"This means I can save money faster to get my own place. And you can have your house back all to yourself."

Pat blinked. "Uh-huh."

Not knowing what else she could say to elicit an actual response, Ronnie just shook her head and continued back to her room. Hurt coursed through her, and she hated it. If only she didn't care as much as Pat clearly didn't.

She had no idea that Pat was no happier than she was.

Chapter 5

Ronnie never thought she would be so nervous on her first day of being a mere receptionist. But then again, she never thought she'd actually *be* a mere receptionist.

She was a ball of nerves from the moment her alarm went off. It wasn't the position she was nervous about, it was what having the position would help her do: get out of her dad's house. Most of every check was going to go right into her savings account. She had already begun browsing apartments.

As usual, Pat was already up, having had his breakfast already. He was sitting at the table, reading a newspaper. They didn't acknowledge each other as Ronnie shuffled over to the refrigerator, frowning as she noticed that all of her produce had been pushed to the back behind Pat's many containers of leftovers. Biting her tongue, she reached behind his things to get to hers, going about the business of making her breakfast. She joined him at the table with her green smoothie, scrolling through news sites on her phone. Pat didn't even look at her. He just continued sipping his coffee and reading.

Realizing she was too wound up to eat, Ronnie went to put the rest of her smoothie in the fridge, but there was practically nowhere to put it. The more she looked at the many containers of leftovers that Pat was probably not going to eat, the more fed up she got. Finally, she slammed the refrigerator door shut and whirled around to face Pat.

"You know, it would be nice if you would leave some room for my things in the refrigerator," she spat.

Pat sat his coffee cup on the table. "You got room."

"*No*, I don't. It's all being taken up by this food that you're clearly not going to eat. I don't know why you always cook so much every night, anyway. It's like you're saving it for someone or something. And we both know it's not for me."

Pat's jaw clenched as he glared at her. "You need to watch yo' mouth."

"What did I say that was disrespectful? All I'm asking is that you leave some room for me in here."

"Like I said, you *got* room! And I can take up all the space I want to; it's *my* 'frigerator!"

"Yes, I know it's your refrigerator. Just like it's *your* TV and *your* couch and *your* house and *your* own special section of the universe. I'm not trying to say anything isn't yours; I'm simply asking for you to make some room for me in your space. Is that so unreasonable?"

Pat blinked. "I made room. You in here, ain't ya? Nothing in this house has ever been good enough for ya and I see it still ain't."

"Where do you get *that*? Just from me asking for some space to put my fruits and vegetables? Or for questioning why in the world you make enough food for an army when you're the only one that's gonna be eating it? I mean, really, you're still cooking like you did back when..."

Her eyes widened and Pat quickly looked away. She had never seen him look so uncomfortable. It was clear a nerve was hit.

"Dad, I—"

"You've said enough." His face turned away, he hurried back to his room, bumping her shoulder as he passed.

Ronnie stood there and watched him hurry away from her as if she had threatened him with a knife. She glanced at the refrigerator then in the direction Pat had escaped to, sinking down into a chair with her head swimming.

It took a gargantuan effort, but Ronnie managed to shake off the kitchen showdown with Pat and focus on her first day of work at Tess's salon, Fierce and 'Fro. After she changed into her lime green work shirt, Tess introduced her to the staff and showed her where everything was, then walked her through how to work the phones and scheduling system. Ronnie already knew she was going to mess up at least once or twice, but Tess assured her that everyone was there to help.

"If you're confused about something, all you have to do is ask," Tess let her know. "We're family around here."

Ronnie smiled tightly. "That's good to know, thanks."

After Tess left her to prepare for the day's clients, Ronnie rubbed her hands together nervously, releasing a shaky breath. She gave herself a little pep talk as she tried to remember everything Tess told her.

As the work day got going, Ronnie tried to settle into her new role. She greeted clients as they came in, offered them juice or water, set appointments and answered the phone. There were a few times where she had to ask someone for clarification on something, but everyone was really nice and eager to help her. Ronnie was grateful for that; she got enough antagonism at home.

"Y'all gon' watch *Empire* tonight?" Tameka, one of the stylists, asked. Ronnie marveled at how she could do such neat cornrows with her long red nails. "Cookie was on one last week, wasn't she?"

"Cookie is *always* on one, but I didn't like her hair last week." Vanessa, the braiding specialist, shook her head. "They could've done better than that."

"You say that about everybody's hair."

"Girl, forget about the hair. Andre was looking yummier than a plate full of neckbones," Tess said with a wink. "Just give me an hour at the Hilton with that man..."

"Didn't you say that last week about Lenny Kravitz?"

"I surely did. It still applies."

Everyone laughed. Ronnie just shook her head and continued scrolling through Zillow listings on the computer. If there was one thing she wasn't interested in, it was salon gossip. She found it silly and juvenile. Whenever someone would try to include her in the conversation, she would politely just smile or give some short answer, excusing herself from inclusion. She was only there to work, not giggle and cackle like a bunch of teenagers.

Towards the end of the day, Tess came over and playfully rapped her knuckles on the desk. "Hey, girl."

Ronnie looked up with the tight smile that was practically automatic now. "Hey, Tess. You need me to do something?"

"Oh no, you're good; the last couple of clients are almost done." Tess leaned onto the desk, her huge breasts spilling over the edge. "So...how did your first day go? Ready to quit yet?"

"Not at all. I really appreciate being here."

"Well good, 'cause everyone already likes you more than that last heffah that sat here. All she did was look down her nose at everybody, acting like she was doing us all a favor just by being here. You know the type, girl; she just stayed in her own little world, not wanting to engage with anybody." She eyed Ronnie, then broke into a smile. "But thank God you're not like that, right?"

Ronnie swallowed and tried to keep her face as even as possible. "Right."

"A couple of us are going out for drinks after we close up. You wanna come?"

"Oh, uh...thanks so much for the invitation, Tess, but I really need to get home tonight. Gotta help my dad with some stuff. But next time." She pulled the keyboard closer to her.

"Cool." Tess tapped the desk again and stood up. "We'll catch you next time. Have a good night. And, hey."

Ronnie looked at her.

"Good job today. I'm glad you're here, Ronnie."

Surprised at the relief that washed over her, Ronnie gave her first actual smile of the day. "I appreciate that, Tess; I actually needed to hear that."

Once Ronnie was in her car, though, she wished she had taken Tess up on her offer to hang out. She had no place else to go, and didn't want to spend money on things like movies or museums. The more she saved, the sooner she could get out of her dad's house, so back to her bedroom and YouTube.

She pulled up to the house, but couldn't make herself get out of the car. As far as she was concerned, this chasm that existed between her and Pat was impenetrable. They had never been very close and it seemed he was not interested in changing that.

Everything in Ronnie wanted to call Edward; he was the only one who really knew what she had gone through with Pat. He had been like her counselor, patiently listening as she unloaded years' worth of frustration about her upbringing. The only bright spot had been Missy, but she was no longer there. Edward had been her sole source of love, affection, and support, and she missed that already. Ronnie wished there was something she could say to make him reconsider their divorce.

She started to dial the number, but stopped herself. It was better to leave well enough alone while they were still on somewhat amicable terms. She didn't want to bug him to the point of annoyance. He might end up changing his number and she wouldn't be able to reach him at all.

Hesitating, she opened her voicemail and listened to a message she had come to rely on a lot in the past few years, as painful as it was to listen to:

"I'll be back soon. Love you, my Ronnie."

Missy had called one day out of the blue, and Ronnie missed it because she was too busy explaining to Edward why she didn't want to go to a party at his friend's house with him. She saw the call come in, but ignored it. When she finally listened to the voicemail and heard it was Missy, she frantically tried to call the number back, but it was restricted. Every day since, she kicked herself for missing that phone call.

The tears came quickly and once they started, Ronnie couldn't stop them. So she just buried her face in her hands and let them out.

Chapter 6

After several more days, things in the Duncan household weren't much better than when Ronnie moved in.

The only time they communicated was when they argued. There was no conversation. Pat still treated Ronnie like an encroacher and Ronnie still behaved as if being in his house was some kind of punishment. Whenever Ronnie would try to make some small effort, like making him a bowl of oatmeal or rearranging things so they made more sense, he would be anything but appreciative.

"I done told you to quit coming in here changing stuff!" he roared. Ronnie had shifted the coffee table when she was cleaning it, which she had learned to do when Pat was out of the house. She only moved the table because she thought it would provide better spacing in the room, but Pat didn't even listen to her reasoning.

"I was only trying to help!" Ronnie insisted. "Why does something this insignificant have to be such a big deal?"

"I got stuff like I have it for a reason!"

"So, what, that means nothing can ever change?"

"When I wanna change somethin', I'll change it. Ain't nothin' wrong with keepin' stuff the way it is."

Yeah, that's probably the very attitude that drove Mama right out the door. It was on the tip of Ronnie's tongue to say, but she didn't want to intentionally antagonize him. She just went to her room without another word.

The next night, Ronnie came home from work to see Pat making a big meal of liver and onions, fried okra, turnip greens, baked potatoes and cornbread. When Ronnie saw this, she tried to keep her automatic frustration in check. She told Pat when she left that morning that she would be making a nice vegetable soup for the both of them when she got home. He clearly disregarded that.

Fuming, Ronnie started to storm off to her room, but she stopped. She wasn't going to let it go this time.

"You know, Dad, it would be really nice if you showed me a little more respect," she stated with a firm jut of her chin.

After an incredulous pause, Pat slowly turned to her. "'Cuse me?"

"I told you that I would make dinner when I got home, and I know you heard me. Yet here you are, making another one of your artery-clogging meals without any regard for me or what I might want whatsoever. It's rude."

"Just like it's rude to tell me that you're making me something without botherin' to ask if it's something I even like or not, which I don't. Don't nobody want no vegetable soup. But just 'cause you think I should be eatin' it, I'm just supposed to take it. *That's* rude."

"Did you ever stop to think I might be doing that for your own good? You *have* to know that eating like you do isn't good for you, regardless of how much you might enjoy it or how many years you've been doing it. At some point you have to take some responsibility and make some changes. Just because you're used to it doesn't make it right."

"Maybe you oughta take your own advice, then, 'cause you ain't always right, either."

Ronnie gaped. "I never said I was!"

"You don't have to say it; ya act like it. You one a' those young folks that think you always know better than us old folks. Well, being young don't make you no genius."

"I don't claim to be a genius, Dad. But you can't even remember to lock the front door half the time. And when it comes to this, I *do* know what's best for you."

"Just like you knew what was best for that husband a' yours, huh?"

Ronnie reeled as though he had slapped her, which is what it felt like. "Wow. That was low, Dad. You didn't have to say that."

"If you treated him anything like you treat me, I see why he put ya out. Everything ain't about you and what *you* like. It's high time somebody told ya that."

"Well, maybe its high time someone told *you* that sometimes change is necessary. That life is about growing and learning and evolving, not being stuck in the same ways you've been in for years."

"If I ain't hurtin' nobody, what's it to ya?"

"It's hurting *you*, Dad!" Ronnie exclaimed. "Whether you realize it or not. Maybe I do tend to think my way is best. But being so closed-minded isn't good, either. Never wanting to listen to anyone else's suggestions or opinions is just another way of making it all about *you*."

Pat considered her words, but only acknowledged them with a grunt, refusing to admit the merit to her words. He just lifted the lid on the pot with the turnip greens and stirred them slowly.

Tears were running down Ronnie's face, and she let them. In that moment, she wanted to be closer to her father; she knew that Missy would be devastated to see their relationship as contentious as it was.

Several quiet moments passed. Pat wouldn't look at his daughter, and Ronnie hoped that what she said pierced something in him enough so he would let her in, even a little bit.

After realizing that he wasn't going to speak, Ronnie sighed wearily. She wiped her eyes with her fingertips, slowly rubbing in the moisture as she tried to calm her surging heartbeat.

"I'm gonna care about you, Dad. Whether you like it or not."

She went to her room, and Pat slowly hung his head.

Ronnie was on her laptop in the living room when there was a knock on the door. She glanced towards the back of the house where Pat was, and hearing no movement, she sighed and set her laptop aside. Trying not to be annoyed that Pat once again didn't let her know that he was expecting company, she trudged to the door and peeked through the side window, automatically wishing she was anywhere else but there.

"Uncle Alvin," she droned, finally swinging open the door.

"My favorite niece," Alvin greeted with a wide smile and open arms.

Instead of allowing him to hug her, Ronnie turned and started to walk off. "Dad is in the back. I'll let him know you're here."

"Ronnie, what a second." When she slowly turned towards him, he asked, "Why is it that you're always so cold towards me?"

She shook her head. "You have some nerve."

"I try to always be kind to you. Especially since I know my brother isn't the warmest blanket in the bin. I'd think you'd appreciate some genuine love and affection, especially since your husband left you."

Her face tightening, Ronnie said through clenched teeth, "That is *none* of your business."

"I wasn't saying that to be ugly. I personally can't imagine why any man would leave such a beautiful, educated woman such as yourself. There must be something wrong with him."

"Uh-huh. Well, thanks. Like I said, I'll go tell Dad you're here."

She turned to leave, but Alvin quickly crossed the room and grabbed her arm. "Ronnie, I think you and I need to talk."

Anger surged through her in the blink of an eye. She snatched her arm away, her eyes shooting daggers.

"Do *not* grab on me like that!"

"Why are you always avoiding me?"

"You need to keep your hands to yourself. I am a grown woman now. I don't have to be around you if I don't want to."

"Ronnie-"

"I didn't know you were in here."

They both turned to see Pat enter the room. Alvin immediately straightened his expression, but Ronnie's frown remained.

"Just got here, brother," Alvin informed. "You ready to play some cards?"

"Yeah, I'm ready. We gon' eat first, though."

"Cool." He looked at his fuming niece. "You wanna join us, Ronnie?"

"No. I do not." She turned and left the room without another word.

Once she was behind the door of her bedroom, Ronnie anxiously paced back and forth across the worn carpet, her skin actually tingling. She mindlessly rubbed her arm where Alvin grabbed her. Visions of punching him in the face danced through her head.

She grabbed her phone, intending to call Edward. Then just as instantly, she remembered that was no longer an option for her. Journaling or doing some kind of physical activity wasn't going to cut it. She was itching to confide in someone, to unload all of the things that were stacking up on her chest. If she didn't, she felt like she might explode.

Her mind whirled and landed on Tess. Maybe if Tess was willing to hang out with her after work, that would mean she'd be willing to listen to her vent, too.

Before she lost her nerve, she dug Tess's business card out of her wallet and dialed the number, shifting her weight and biting her lip. Part of her hoped Tess wouldn't pick up but the larger part prayed that she would.

"Hello?"

"Tess, hey..."

"Ronnie? What's up, you sound strange. Everything okay?"

Ronnie opened her mouth to unload, but felt herself clamming up before anything came out. Just that quickly, she regretted the decision to call Tess. This woman was someone she didn't really have a relationship with at all, and more importantly, Tess was now her boss. How would she look calling her out of the blue and crying about her personal business? She felt foolish for thinking Tess would even care to hear it.

"Uh, yeah," she finally said. "I'm sorry to call you so late..."

"It's just nine o'clock."

"Still...it was wrong of me to call."

"You don't hear me fussing about that. What's going on?"

"Nothing. I just...wanted to know if you all like doughnuts. I thought I could bring some Krispy Kremes for everybody one day soon."

"Hell yeah we like doughnuts. Especially Krispy Kreme. Girl, you bring some of those up in there and they'll put you in their will."

Ronnie couldn't help but chuckle a little. This was another reason why she thought Tess would be a good person to call;

she was so easygoing and funny that she made Ronnie forget about whatever was bothering her, if only for a few moments. Why else would she volunteer to buy something with her limited funds that she didn't even eat herself?

But try as she might, she couldn't make herself start talking. As cool as Tess seemed, Ronnie just didn't quite trust her. What was to stop her from blabbing Ronnie's business to the ladies at the salon? Ronnie heard how they liked to gossip. Most of it seemed limited to famous people and not anyone they knew personally, but who's to say that's how it always was? Ronnie had only been working there a short time; she probably hadn't seen or heard everything they usually did yet. There was no way she wanted her failed marriage or turbulent relationship with her father to be the next topic of discussion on the salon floor.

"I'll keep that in mind, then," she finally said. "I've gotta go...sorry again to bother you."

"No bother. Feel free to call whenever you need to."

"Okay, thanks. Good night."

Ronnie ended the call feeling ridiculous, and alone.

Chapter 7

It hadn't been the best day at work. Ever since Ronnie rolled out of bed that morning, she felt irritable and off-kilter. The last thing she felt like doing was going to work, but she was no more eager to stay home with Pat and his sullen attitude.

So she put on the ridiculous lime green shirt and sucked it up, doing her job and nothing more. She could only manage to give just enough to everyone; just enough professionalism to clients, just enough pleasantries to coworkers. Salon gossip had never interested her and she was even less interested today.

"Hey Ronnie, come over here," Vanessa called out. "We wanna get your opinion on something."

"Can it wait a second?" Ronnie responded, trying not to sound as annoyed as she was. "I'm updating something on the calendar."

"Girl, that's not going anywhere. You can finish it in a few minutes. Come on."

With a sigh she hoped the others didn't notice, Ronnie pushed herself away from the receptionist desk and wandered to the main floor. Vanessa, Tess, Tameka, Rhoda, and Raja the manicurist, were huddled around the latest issue of Ebony, debating something amongst themselves. There were no customers in the salon at the moment, and in those instances the ladies turned up the grown-woman talk. Ronnie figured they were going to ask her opinion on someone's false eyelashes or the imprint in some guy's gray sweatpants.

"Where do you think would be the better place for a girl's trip?" Tameka asked her. She pointed to a picture of a beautiful beach on an island that Ronnie knew she had never been to, even though she had no idea where it was. "Me and Rhoda think that this place in the Bahamas would be perfect. Nice, serene, relaxing..."

"And typical," Vanessa interjected. "*I* think we should go somewhere less obvious, like the Netherlands or Egypt. Make it a real adventure."

Tess sucked her teeth. "Yeah, whatever. I'm not trying to spend the little vacation time I get being adventurous. Heck, I'd be cool going to Vegas or Cali or somewhere."

"Take me to Ghana any day," Raja chimed in. "We all could use a little culture."

"Which one would you choose, Ronnie?" Tess asked.

All eyes turned to Ronnie. She didn't like being put on the spot, even though she wasn't any more eager to ponder vacation destinations when she wouldn't be going on them herself.

"They all sound nice," she said with a light shrug. "All of you are going together?"

"Yeah. We try to do something together every year. Kind of a team building, bonding kinda thing, you know? Plus, it's just good to get away and have fun with your girls."

I wouldn't know. "Oh. Well yeah, any one of those would be good." She breathed an internal sigh of relief when the front desk phone rang. "I better get that," she mumbled before scurrying away.

The day continued, and Ronnie was counting down the minutes until she could get out of there. She just wanted to be by herself. She was sweeping the waiting area when Tess called her to the back.

"Is something wrong?" Ronnie asked, once they were in Tess's office.

"Unfortunately yes, it is." Tess sighed, adjusting her huge hoop earrings. "Hopefully, though, it's something we can nip in the bud."

Ronnie frowned, confused. "What is it?"

"Well, there's no cute way to say this so I'm just gonna spill it. Your attitude is turning people off."

"Wh-what?"

"You're standoffish, you don't engage; you give off this vibe like you can't be bothered with anybody. And it's not going over very well with my staff."

"Oh..." Ronnie's face flushed. "Are you about to fire me?"

"No, of course not," Tess quickly assured her. "But I *do* want to bring it to your attention because hopefully it's something that you just don't realize you're doing. I told you, we're all family here. And while I'm not saying you have to be everybody's BFF, we can't have someone in here that brings bad energy. That's just not gonna work."

Ronnie *hadn't* wanted to be bothered, but she didn't think it was so obvious that she didn't. She thought she was being pleasant enough. But apparently being just pleasant *wasn't* enough.

"I-I'm sorry, Tess. I didn't mean to give off bad vibes. I'll work on that, I promise."

"It's almost as if you think of this place as some kind of punishment or something. And it's far from that. This isn't community service. You don't *have* to be here."

Her face on fire, Ronnie nodded. "I know."

"Ronnie, is something going on with you? I've been getting the feeling that you're going through something pretty big, even more so after you called me the other night. I'm not trying to get in your business, I swear. But I'm a great listener. And whatever you tell me will stay between you and me."

Ronnie wanted to open up. She ached to. She believed Tess had good intentions. And she was impartial enough to give unbiased feedback.

"Okay, I admit I *am* going through some major stuff," Ronnie admitted. She hastily crossed her arms. "Apparently I'm not doing a good job of leaving my issues at the door."

"Girl, you're human; it's not always easy to shrug everything off just because you're at work. But keeping everything bottled up isn't good, either. Getting things off your chest might make you feel better; unburden you a little bit."

"You're probably right. And please don't take my hesitancy to open up about all of this stuff personally-"

"Not at all." Tess smiled at her, placing a warm hand on her arm briefly. "When and if you're ready, you know how to reach me. In the meantime, try to think of this place as a way to escape all of that for a few hours everyday. Loosen up. It's okay to laugh and be silly sometimes. I know it helps keep me from going crazy, personally."

"That certainly sounds nice."

"When is the last time you laughed, Ronnie? I mean *really* laughed; like tears rolling, stomach hurting, can't-catch-your-breath laughed?"

"Oh, wow...it's been a while, I admit." And it had. Now that the question had been asked, Ronnie was racking her brain trying to recall the last time she did anything more than just chuckle at something. There just hadn't been very much to laugh at in her life recently.

"Honey, life is just too short to go through without laughing," Tess advised. "There's plenty of bad stuff going on out there. In here, it's a refuge. People come in here to look good, feel good, and get away from all the world's foolishness. You just have to open yourself up to it."

Ronnie pulled into the Walmart parking lot. She took a few minutes to calculate exactly how much she wanted to spend and check sales prices on her phone before getting out of the car. Her mind was still on everything that had been going on as she grabbed a cart, disinfected the handlebar with the provided wipes, and trudged towards the produce section. Checking her watch, she hoped to be in and out in no more than thirty minutes.

"How are you today?" a male voice said from behind her.

Figuring they were speaking to someone else, Ronnie ignored it and continued dropping zucchini into a produce bag.

"Excuse me, miss...you, with the braids."

Glancing to either side of her and seeing no one else with braids, Ronnie looked over her shoulder, clearly surprised. An attractive man with skin the color of a sweet potato stood there smiling at her.

"Yes?"

"I'm Charleston; not trying to disturb you but I couldn't resist speaking."

Ronnie frowned slightly. "Why is that?"

"'Cause I find you incredibly attractive."

"Oh..." Ronnie hadn't expected that. She couldn't remember the last time she was approached by a man. "Um...thanks."

"What's your name?"

She hesitated slightly. "Ronnie."

"It's nice to meet you, Ronnie."

"Thanks. I don't mean to be rude or anything, but I'm kind of in a hurry."

"No problem; I don't wanna hold you up." He smiled at her. "Hopefully we'll run into each other again when you have more time."

"Right. Um, thanks." Dropping the zucchini into her cart, Ronnie quickly pushed her cart away, feeling awkward. The last thing she needed was to get involved with anyone else. All she knew as far as relationships was Edward, and their divorce wasn't even final. Part of her was still holding out hope that he would change his mind and take her back, even though she knew that was a long shot. The only communication they had since she last saw him was when he had the divorce papers sent to Pat's house. She still had yet to sign them.

Ronnie wandered down the necessary aisles, gathering the things on her list and keeping an eye out for her unwanted admirer. Whenever she passed by someone, she couldn't resist looking into their carts and critiquing their choices. It amazed her how many people didn't seem to care more about their own health, their purchases consisting of processed foods, meats, and sugary stuff. She itched to tell them what that kind of stuff did to their bodies, but refrained. If they didn't care, why should she?

When she had everything she needed, she went to the front to check out. As usual, most of the lanes were closed and the few that were open had lines four or five people deep. She opted for the self-checkout, and tapped her fingers impatiently on the cart handlebar as she waited her turn. Charleston ended up behind her, and he gave her a bright smile. She flashed a quick, tight-lipped semi-smile in return and turned forward, hating that he chose to come stand behind her. Had he been watching her this whole time, waiting to get another chance to hit on her? Thankfully, he didn't say anything to her and she prayed that continued, because she simply was not interested.

She quickly went to the next available checkout and starting ringing up her purchases, hoping there would be room for everything in the refrigerator. When the total came to a little more than she budgeted for, she opted to use her rarely-used credit card instead of putting some things back. Edward had given it to her a while back for emergencies, and she figured this was close enough.

Her skin burned with embarrassment, though, when she slid the card and it came up as declined. Quickly looking around her to see if anyone noticed, Ronnie fumed. Despite what they were going through, Ronnie sincerely thought that Edward would throw her this small bone of letting her keep her credit card. Oftentimes she forgot she even had it, she used it so rarely. But apparently Edward hadn't.

"Everything okay?"

She jumped when she heard Charleston's voice and wondered if he saw the declined message on the machine. Quickly trying to cover the screen with her hand, she feigned a casual shrug.

"Yeah. Just...accidentally grabbed the wrong card, that's all. This one is expired." She jabbed the button with her thumb to clear the message and grudgingly yanked her debit card from her wallet.

"You sure? I can help you out, if you need it. Let me get this for you."

"Oh, no. That's okay."

"I don't mind. We all need help sometimes. Nothing to be embarrassed about."

"That's very kind of you but I got it."

"Okay, then. If you insist."

Ronnie quickly finished paying for her groceries, then threw the bags into her card and hustled out of the store without looking back. She was fuming. While Edward had told her point blank that he was cutting off all ties to her, for whatever reason she didn't think that included her credit card. It's not like it had a high limit; it was only five hundred bucks. But Edward clearly had all of his bases covered, not leaving any wiggle room for a reason for Ronnie to have to reach out to him. He really was cutting her off completely, and the reminder of that made her heart burn.

When she got back to Pat's, she dumped her groceries onto the kitchen table and hurried to her room, tearing into the still-packed boxes for anything that Edward had ever given her. Tears streamed down her face as she threw any gift, article of clothing, or anything else to the floor, destroying anything she could manage to with her bare hands. Pictures of them, birthday or anniversary cards, love letters, the movie stub from their first date; all ripped to shreds. Any clothes she had bought with his money got tossed to the floor. All of their tangible memories, Ronnie wanted out of her sight. She didn't take the time to think how she might regret what she was doing later; her anger had taken over. If Edward could throw her and their relationship away like it was nothing, she should do the same.

Finally, she dropped down onto the bed, surveying the chaos in front of her. When she realized that she wasn't left with much after getting rid of everything from Edward, a new wave of anger washed over her. What had she been thinking, being so dependent on him? When she and Edward fell in love, he promised to take care of her. And after they married, he told her she only needed to work if she wanted to; he loved her being there when he got home every day. So Ronnie fell into being a housewife; a kept woman. It didn't cross her mind what might happen if she and Edward ever split up, because she never thought it would happen. She thought he was the one person that would never leave her, and she clung to him, not even trying to have anything for herself outside of their cozy little household. Now, she realized how foolish that was.

She just sat there crying, looking at the mess in front of her and thinking about the mess her life was. There was no way she would have predicted this in a million years. She had no mother, no marriage, no real relationship with her father and no plan for her life. The realization humiliated her and brought a fresh wave of tears.

She heard footsteps coming down the hall and quickly wiped her eyes, hating that she hadn't closed her bedroom door before going on her Edward-purging frenzy. Knowing she wouldn't be able to hide everything before her dad saw it, she just turned her head away, hoping he wouldn't pay her any attention and walk right by her.

Pat did notice. He paused at the doorway to her room, looking at all the mess, noting the types of items that had been destroyed, then at her. She kept her eyes averted, anxiously rocking back and forth as she bit her lip, trying to prevent more tears from falling. Pat walked off without a word and Ronnie hung her head, both appreciating and hating that.

Moments later, Pat reappeared, a large trashcan in hand. He wordlessly placed it just on the inside of the door, then walked off.

Ronnie just looked at the trashcan in surprise, feeling increasingly overwhelmed with gratitude at the gesture. Despite everything, a small smile crept to her lips.

"Thanks, Dad," she whispered.

Chapter 8

"They said it might rain today; can't forget my umbrella. You know how you are about wet clothes."

Pat adjusted his tie as he got ready for church. He was in a hurry since he overslept, which was something he rarely did. A bad dream had caused his sleep to be restless, and he didn't get up in time to make himself breakfast like he usually did. He went straight into the shower, thankful that he had already laid out his clothes for the day. And Missy's, of course.

"Guess I'll grab some juice or something for breakfast since I don't have time to fix anything," he muttered, shrugging on his suit jacket. "Don't fuss at me; this the first time I overslept in years. I promise I'll have something proper later on."

When he emerged from his bedroom, he wasn't surprised to see Ronnie stretched out in the living room, doing her yoga. He had come to expect it, having learned she liked to do yoga on Sunday mornings. Ever since their initial blow-up, Ronnie was very careful of how she moved the furniture, taking great care not to disrupt any of Missy's things. Pat appreciated this, though silently, as he maneuvered around the furniture, not realizing when he had gotten used to Ronnie's usual temporary rearrangement.

He went to the refrigerator for some juice but stopped short, noticing a plate on the table covered in plastic wrap. Stepping over to peer at it, he saw it was some form of bacon, potatoes, and some white scrambled eggs. A banana laid next to it.

Ronnie appeared in the doorway, giving him a tentative smile. She motioned towards the plate. "When I got up and saw you were still asleep, I figured I'd try to save you some time and make your breakfast."

He looked at her.

"This is all stuff I've seen you eat before; just healthier versions of it…scrambled egg whites, roasted potatoes, and veggie bacon. I know you've probably never had veggie bacon before, but hopefully you'll give it a try." Her smile widened slightly. "It's very good, though I don't expect for you to like it as much as the pork kind."

Her eyes were hopeful. Pat realized the effort she was making, and felt himself appreciating it.

"I 'preciate that," he said, sincere. He glanced at his watch. "If I sit and try to eat this now, though, I'll be late."

Ronnie's face fell slightly.

"But I'll have it when I get back, if ya don't mind."

Brightening, Ronnie graced him with a full smile. It was probably the first one since she had come back to stay with him. Pat couldn't help but notice how pretty her smile was; how much it looked like Missy's.

"Not at all," Ronnie said. "I'll put it in the refrigerator for you."

Pat grabbed the banana. "This'll hold me over 'til later."

Clearly pleased, Ronnie grinned, relieved. She wanted to make something for Pat that he liked, but couldn't bring herself to fry anything like he was used to. So she prayed this compromise worked, fully preparing herself for him to toss the whole plate in the trash. But thankfully, he hadn't.

Letting her know he'd be back later, Pat headed out. He felt a lightness he didn't usually feel, and could only wonder if that was due to the pleasant exchange with his daughter. There hadn't been many, even before she moved back in. Pat couldn't deny that it was nice not to fuss with her for a change.

He got to church just before service started, grateful that no one was in his usual seat in the fifth row on the right side. After so many years, the members knew he liked to sit in that spot, close to the wall. Pat enjoyed the service, his voice a little louder when he sang along with the choir and his occasional grunts and 'Amens' more fervent. When it was time for prayer, his eyes squeezed shut on their own, praying for the usual things but also giving thanks for what he already had, something he realized he didn't do much of.

But when he saw his sister-in-law Debra approach him afterwards, that familiar anxiety swarmed over him like a family of ants.

"How are you, Pat?" she greeted him with her usual hug.

"Can't complain."

"It's so good to see you."

"You, too."

Without further preamble, Debra reached into her purse and pulled out another postcard from Missy. Pat released a breath as he ran his fingers over the few words in Missy's handwriting, it as usual leaving no clue as to where she was, only that she was okay. A slight frown creased his brow.

Debra noticed. "You okay?"

Searching for the right words, Pat finally responded, "I don't know how much more of this I can take."

His words surprised him, but not Debra. Nodding in understanding, she placed a hand on his arm. "You have been as patient as anybody can expect, Pat."

"But she's my wife."

"And she's my sister. I love her as much as I always did, but she chose to leave without a word to anyone. We can't put our lives on hold forever. It's been twenty years already."

Pat nodded, his eyes still on the postcard as if waiting for answers. "Sometimes it don't seem that long."

"Well, it's been an eternity for me. Our parents died without ever seeing her again; part of me is angry with her for that. The truth is, we may never know where she is or why she left."

Pat winced at those words, even though the same thought had crossed his mind several times over the years, no matter how much he tried to suppress it. Every day he prayed for Missy to come back. Every day he wondered if he had done something to make her leave in the first place. He had tried to be a good husband to her, though he knew he wasn't perfect. Having so many unanswered questions weighing on him for long, not knowing if he was ever going to get the answers, was causing him to grow weary.

"If you want to move on, Pat, you should." Her hand was still on his arm. "Not one person would think less of you."

Pat didn't like that thought. He didn't want to give up on Missy. The thought had never crossed his mind in twenty years.

"I never said othing' 'bout movin' on," he grumbled, slightly offended at the suggestion.

"Pat." She waited for him to look at her. "Are you happy?"

He wasn't. But he had resigned himself to not being happy. "Life ain't 'bout being happy all the time."

"Then what in the world is it about? Why be miserable if you don't have to be?"

Pat didn't know how to respond, so he just turned his eyes back to the postcard.

Several moments passed before Debra spoke again. "Look, why don't you come to the house and get something to eat. I already cooked a nice pot roast with potatoes and I can't eat all that by myself."

Even though he certainly knew what it was like to cook too much, Pat hesitated. "I should probably get on home."

"And do what, sit watching baseball? I know how much you love your Braves. You can watch that at my house, Pat. It would just be nice to have some company for a change."

Pat thought about Ronnie. They hadn't made any plans, but he did tell her he'd eat the breakfast she made for him later. But that didn't mean he couldn't make a stop on the way home. For all he knew, Ronnie wouldn't even be there when he got back. Her breakfast would still be there when he got home.

"I guess I can come over there for a lil' while," he finally relented.

"Wonderful!" Debra grinned, and for the first time he noticed just how much she resembled her older sister. Pat realized he had never *really* looked at her before.

He followed Debra to her house, all the while wondering why he was going. This wasn't part of his routine, and it felt strange. He always went straight home after church, changed clothes, then kicked back on the couch with a beer, watching whatever sport was on TV. He loved them all. Missy could only stand to watch with him for a while before she got tired of it, but he could watch all day.

After Debra heated up the food, the two of them sat at her round dinner table and ate, not talking much at first. Pat didn't know what to say; he and Debra had always got along fine, but they hadn't spent any one-on-one time together before then.

"Didn't your daughter come back to stay with you?" Debra finally asked.

Pat cleared his throat. "Yeah."

"Goodness, I haven't seen Ronnie in years," Debra marveled, her expression clearly trying to recall the last time she laid eyes on her niece. "How is everything going with you two?"

"It's going all right. Well as can be expected, considerin'."

"You two aren't very close, huh?"

Pat wondered if there was judgement in her tone. "Not really."

"Is that how you like it?"

"That's just always been the way it is. She was always closer to her mama."

"In all this time you two haven't tried to improve things between you? How old is she now?"

Pat paused, momentarily unsure. "Thirty-five, I believe."

"Now is as good a time as any, Pat," Debra advised. "She's grown, staying with you..."

"Only 'cause she has to."

"Whatever the reason is, she's there. Take advantage of the opportunity. Whether or not either of you want to admit it, you need each other."

Pat just stuck another hunk of pot roast into his mouth, not responding. He would be willing to bet that Ronnie would deny needing him in a heartbeat, for anything other than a place to stay. He knew that as soon as she saved enough money, she'd be out of there and they'd be right back to where they were before, each acting as if the other didn't exist.

Eventually they migrated to the living room. Pat was feeling slightly more at ease, finding Debra rather easy to talk to. She turned on the Braves game as promised, but they ended up not paying much attention to it as their conversation continued.

"Why do you think you and Ronnie have so much distance between you?" Debra asked, curling her stockinged feet underneath her on the couch. Pat was sitting on the other end.

"I can admit I wanted a son," Pat replied. "When they told us we was havin' a girl, I couldn't make myself be that happy 'bout it. I tried, but couldn't."

"Is that why you named her Ronnie?"

"Yeah. If she had been a boy, we was gon' name her Ronald."

"I'm surprised Missy agreed to that. When we were kids, she used to always talk about the girly names she would choose for her daughter, like Rose or Tiffany."

"She didn't care either way. She was so over the moon when Ronnie was born, she wasn't worried 'bout what we named her. Plus, she knew I wanted a boy."

"Does Ronnie know that?"

Pat shrugged. "Don't know. I ain't never told her. Why?"

"I just wonder if maybe that's at least part of the reason why she has so much distance from you. She senses that you didn't want her."

That statement stung Pat. "I never said I didn't want her."

"Okay, well, you resent that she's not a boy."

"Maybe. That, and we don't have nothin' in common."

"How do you know? I bet if you two spent some time getting to know each other better, you'd discover you have things in common. There's probably a ton of things about your daughter that you don't even know."

"Probably. But she ain't interested in that."

"Again I ask, how do you know that? Has she said that point blank?"

"Naw, not point blank. We don't talk much. Actions speak louder than words, anyway."

"That's true, but Pat...don't you think it's finally time to make the effort to get closer to your daughter? She's in her mid-thirties, you're no spring chicken yourself..."

"I'm aware."

"Don't let any more time pass, is my point. Tomorrow isn't promised to any of us. How would you feel if something happened to Ronnie with things between you the way they are?"

It was something Pat never thought of, but now that the question had been raised, it blared through his mind like a siren. Of course he wouldn't want anything to happen to Ronnie, regardless of how strained their relationship was. He wondered if she could say the same about him.

They sat and talked while half-watching the game a while longer before Pat decided it was time for him to go. When he glanced at his watch, he realized he had been there for almost three hours.

"Thank you for coming by, Pat," Debra said as she walked him to the door. "It was so nice to have someone here to talk to."

"I figured you liked being by yourself."

"Why, 'cause I never married and don't have any children? That's just unfortunate circumstance."

"Unfortunate circumstance?"

"You remember I was engaged to be married about ten years ago, right? My fiancé had a heart attack a week before the wedding."

Pat had forgotten all about that. "Oh yeah. Sorry."

"No need to apologize. But it took me a long time to heal from that. I'll probably never fully get over losing Ted. But eventually I realized that life goes on, and he wouldn't want me moping around feeling sorry for myself forever."

"How come you ain't get with somebody else, then? You ain't bad to look at."

Debra chuckled. She knew that was as close to a compliment from Pat as she would get.

"Thank you. In answer to your question, though, I don't know. I didn't put much effort into it either way. Figured God would send somebody to me when He was ready, I guess. By now I'm just used to being alone."

Pat nodded, understanding. "I know what you mean."

"I know you do." Debra leaned in, embracing him. The hug was firmer than the ones she usually gave him at church. Pat also noticed that she took her time pulling away. He just stood there, not used to another woman being in his arms for this long. Had she been smelling like vanilla all day?

Eventually, Debra eased back. Her honey-brown eyes roamed his face for a moment before she leaned in and gently touched her lips to his, her warm hand touching his face. Pat froze, not knowing what to do. He didn't kiss her back; he hadn't been kissed in over twenty years. But he didn't stop her, either.

The kiss lingered for moments that felt like eternities. Debra moved closer, and Pat's mind noticed the lushness of her body. Breasts, hips and thighs, all things he hadn't felt in years outside of platonic hugs, were now pressed against him and waking up things that Pat thought were forever dead.

He pulled back, guilty. Neither of them needed to look down to know she affected him. She looked at him, silently letting him know it was okay. She smiled, her lips still moist. Part of Pat wanted to continue the kiss, and the thought horrified him.

Embarrassed, he quickly turned to leave without a word.

Chapter 9

Pat didn't realize the slight frown he wore as he watched the baseball game.

He was trying his hardest to put what happened with Debra out of his mind, but it wasn't easy. He could almost still feel her lips against his. Occasionally he would touch where her hand caressed his cheek, and he'd catch himself and frown harder. He simply had no business enjoying that as much as he had. Of all the things he was, a cheater had never been one of them.

Of course, he wasn't going to tell anyone about it. The closest people to him were Ronnie and Alvin. His brother would probably encourage him to do it again, but Ronnie might think he had betrayed Missy. As long as she was alive, there was a chance she could come back. Pat believed that. He just tried to chalk it up to a one-time slip in composure and bury himself in ESPN.

At some point, Ronnie wandered into the living room. She peered at the television for a few moments before sitting on the other end of the couch.

The two of them watched the game for a while in silence.

"Are there supposed to be so many people on the field?" Ronnie eventually asked.

"Hmm?"

"On the field." Ronnie pointed. "Looks like a lot of people."

Pat chuckled, remembering she never had been that into sports. Apparently, that hadn't changed.

"It's nine people out there on defense," he informed her.

"Nine, really? How many in basketball?"

"Ten altogether. Five to a team."

"Didn't you used to play baseball?"

"Yep."

"What did you do?"

"Shortstop."

"What is a shortstop?"

"Guards the area 'tween second and third base."

"Like that guy wearing number seven right there?"

"Yep."

"That seems a long way from home base. You had to throw it all that way?"

"Plenty 'a times."

"Wow."

Ronnie continued to ask questions about what was happening and Pat answered them, more amused than anything. Usually he didn't like to be bothered while watching a game, but today he welcomed the distraction. He wondered if it was simply because he was trying to forget what happened with Debra or if he just didn't mind Ronnie's company.

And he figured that Ronnie was making an effort, since she probably was no more a baseball fan than she used to be. But he was, so she was showing an interest. He thought that was nice of her.

After several more questions, Ronnie quieted down and watched the game. Pat waited for her to get up and retreat back to her bedroom, but she never did. She stayed for the rest of the game, only getting up to get some grapes from the kitchen.

It was their first father-daughter time in years.

Ronnie had already given herself several pep talks, reminding herself to loosen up and be more sociable at work. She remembered what Tess said about the salon being a refuge. At least she wasn't somewhere taking orders through a drive-thru window or waiting for someone to count coupons behind a cash register. It was all about looking at the bright side.

"Good morning, Ronnie," Tess called out when Ronnie entered. She was straightening up her booth.

"Hey Tess, good morning." Ronnie stashed her purse behind the receptionist desk before continuing to the salon floor. Vanessa and Raja were also there setting up; Tameka and Rhoda hadn't arrived yet. "Good morning Vanessa, Raja."

"Good mor-*ooooh*! You brought Krispy Kremes??" Vanessa exclaimed, dropping her combs back into the Barbicide she was about to take them out of and rushing over to her.

"Yes, I thought I'd surprise y'all. Hope you haven't eaten already."

"Since when does that matter? Krispy Kremes are automatic," Raja stated. "I want two of 'em, I'm just putting it out there right now."

"What is that, an appetizer? 'Cause you know good and well you eat more than that," Tess quipped with a shake of her head, her afro jiggling.

"You shut up."

"Girl, we all some greedy asses when it comes to these things," Vanessa said with a wave of her hand before taking one of the two boxes from Ronnie. "Thank you, Ronnie! This was so nice of you!"

"My pleasure. Just wanted to do something to show how much I appreciate you all being patient with me." She glanced at Tess, who smiled knowingly.

"It's what we do," she said with a wink, coming to take the other box. "You certainly know how to get on our good side. I'm gonna dig in 'cause my first client will be here in twenty minutes."

"Me too. I'm booked solid today," Raja commented. "And I'm certainly not complaining about it."

"Yep, it's gonna be a busy day so let's get this sugar high rolling and make this money."

"You gonna have some, Ronnie?" Vanessa asked her.

"Oh...no, thank you. I ate breakfast before I left the house so I'm stuffed. But y'all enjoy."

"Oh, we will!"

Ronnie returned to the front desk with a smile on her face, feeling like she had at least broken some ground. Tess had a point before when she said Ronnie had been acting like working there was like a punishment. The fact was, Tess had done her a huge favor by hiring her. Ronnie hadn't worked a day in her life and if she hadn't happened to run into Tess that day, she would probably still be filling out applications and waiting for the phone to ring. And it was time Ronnie began acting more grateful.

Now that she had let her guard down some, she realized that working in a hair salon was actually a pretty cool first job. Ronnie still had no idea what it was she wanted to do with her life; with everything going on, she hadn't sat down to really think about any long-term plans. When she was in college, she majored in sociology, wanting to be an urban and regional planner. But now, her interests had changed...she just didn't know to exactly what yet.

"Ronnie, do you watch American Idol?" Rhoda asked her later in the day.

"I haven't watched that since the Fantasia days."

"Oh damn! Yeah, you're way out of the loop, then," Rhoda laughed.

"I really only still watch it for the bad auditions," Vanessa chimed in, her hands expertly installing some box braids. "After that, I don't bother with it."

"I'm just wondering how many more years they're gonna do it. No matter how many times they change judges, I'm over it." Tess slid a bobby pin into her client's slick, high bun. "After they screwed Jennifer Hudson, I quit watching it, anyway."

"Yeah they did, girl, but she certainly came up after that," Tameka said. "She's got all kinds of awards, endorsements, still acting and singing her behind off."

"What show do you like, Ronnie?" Tess asked her.

"I don't watch a whole lot of TV, really," Ronnie admitted, determined not to give one of her usual short, dismissive answers. "When I do, though, it's usually something on Food Network or HGTV."

"Oh, I love me some Property Brothers!" Raja called out from the manicure table where she was working on a set of acrylics. "I can watch that all day."

"Hell, I need on those people to come make over my place," Vanessa joked. "Anybody on HGTV will do; I ain't picky."

Ronnie laughed. She was actually enjoying herself and kinda hated it when she had to go back over to the receptionist desk to take a call. As soon as she got another chance to, she wandered back to the salon floor, laughing and talking with the stylists and clients. She still wasn't revealing too much about herself, but she was participating in the conversations and sincerely interested in what everyone had to say.

At the end of the day, Ronnie looked forward to getting home and relaxing. It had been a busy day and she just wanted to unwind and veg out.

"Ooh, point me to the nearest bar," Vanessa droned, flopping into her salon chair. She rubbed her neck. "Tess, we need to have a massage therapist up in here."

"That's in the plans," Tess assured her. "Gimme another year or so."

"In the meantime, let's go drown our sorrows in some libations."

"You wanna come, Ronnie?"

"I would, but I can't wait to get home and take a hot shower before losing myself in Netflix."

"I feel you. Well, as soon as we finish getting everything cleaned up, we're gonna head out."

Ronnie finished straightening the waiting area before she picked up her phone. She only hesitated for a second before she called Pat. Since he had been considerate enough to let her know when he was going to get home, she felt it only fair that she do the same. And she knew he didn't text.

"Hey, Dad. I'm going to be headed home in a little while. Just, um, just letting you know."

"That's fine. Alvin might be here by then. We playin' cards again tonight."

"Oh." Ronnie rolled her eyes. "On second thought, I might just go get a drink with my coworkers first. It's been a long day."

There was a pause. "Changed yo' mind that quick, huh?"

"Yes. They asked and I don't want to keep turning them down. Tonight's as good a time as any."

Ronnie knew Pat wasn't blind enough to think that was all there was to it. But thankfully, he didn't press the issue.

"Okay, then," he finally said. "Take care."

"Um, you too."

Ending the call, Ronnie whirled around towards Tess and the girls. "Hey Tess? I think I will go with y'all, after all. I could use a drink."

While Ronnie was out with her coworkers, Pat put the finishing touches on the dinner of stewed chicken thighs and rice he was preparing. His brow was furrowed. Ever since Ronnie's call, he wondered what was going on. She was on her way home until she learned Alvin was coming over, and then she changed her tune. Pat wasn't foolish enough to think that was a coincidence.

When Alvin arrived, they sat down to eat. Pat wasn't saying much.

"I appreciate you cooking, brother, but you know it's fine to just order a pizza sometimes," Alvin commented. "You don't have to keep going through all this trouble just 'cause I'm here."

"I cook everyday whether you here or not. And I don't trust restaurant food."

"We certainly don't have that in common. I eat out or order in almost every night of the week. I don't get a home-cooked meal until I come over here."

"Umph."

Alvin looked at him. "Something on your mind, brother?"

Pat put down his fork. "Why does Ronnie always make herself scarce every time you come 'round?"

Shrugging innocently, Alvin shook his head. "I wish I knew. I was gonna ask *you* that, actually."

"Me?" Pat looked at him skeptically. "How would I know? You know good and well me and Ronnie ain't never been all that close."

"I thought maybe she confided in Missy or something and Missy told you. Speaking of Missy, you said another postcard from her came in, right?"

"Yeah." Thinking of the last postcard made Pat think of who gave it to him, and he stomped the thought out like a flaming newspaper. "And Missy never told me nothin' 'bout you and Ronnie."

"Well, your guess is as good as mine, then."

"So she just don't like you, for *no* reason?"

"It's not unusual, brother. You know how women are. They're emotional and their emotions don't always make sense. Plus, isn't Ronnie getting to menopause age?"

Pat didn't buy that response. "That don't have nothin' to do with her not likin' you."

"I bet it does."

"Back when you used to babysit her, did ya give her some kind of punishment she didn't like? Whip her, tell her she couldn't watch TV..."

"No, nothing like that. We always had a great time together." Alvin looked at him earnestly. "Pat, I'm telling you, whatever problem Ronnie has with me, I'm not in on it."

Pat eyed his brother as Alvin resumed eating his meal. He knew in his gut that Alvin wasn't being honest about something. There were several times that Pat would drop Ronnie off at Alvin's, because Missy was off doing some volunteer work or something for the church, and Pat couldn't be bothered with trying to entertain a little girl. Alvin was always more than happy to watch Ronnie while Pat went to a bar to watch a baseball game, or if Missy managed to drag him along with her wherever she was going. Even when she wanted to take Ronnie with them, Pat convinced her they could move a lot faster if they didn't.

But Alvin had always been a straight-up man; he worked in the public school system and had for the past thirty years. He was a widower, his wife dying of cancer two years into their marriage. Alvin had dated several women since then, but never remarried. He always loved children but didn't have any of his own, so Pat thought it was good for everyone when he took Ronnie to stay with him.

Maybe it was just hormones, Pat surmised. It wasn't impossible. It wasn't like Ronnie was the most welcoming person. She often seemed to have a chip on her shoulder. She wasn't butting heads with Pat as much as she had when she first moved in, but that had taken a while and things still were rather strained occasionally. She probably hadn't spent any time around Alvin in years.

Resuming eating his own meal, Pat decided that all Ronnie and Alvin needed was some time. She'd come around soon enough.

Chapter 10

P at and Ronnie sat at the table, eating breakfast together. Grits and eggs for Pat, avocado toast for Ronnie. Their conversation was pleasant, if somewhat awkward.

"You likin' that job?" Pat asked her. He sipped his coffee.

"I am. It was a little rocky at first but I'm liking it a whole lot more now."

"What is it you do?"

"I'm the receptionist at a hair salon. Answer the phone, make appointments, that kind of stuff."

"That's what you went to college for?"

Ronnie paused, wondering if this was sarcasm. Opting to think positively, she replied, "No, I majored in sociology. But a lot of things are different now."

"Hmm."

"This is just something so I can get back on my feet and make my own money while I figure out what it is I really want to do."

"I see."

"My old classmate owns the salon and was kind enough to give me a shot."

"Give you a shot? It ain't hard to answer the phone, is it?"

"Well, when you've never had a real job, even the simplest things can seem difficult."

"I suppose."

"But don't worry; I'm saving most of my money so hopefully within a year, I'll be able to get out of your hair."

Pat glanced at her briefly, his cinnamon-colored face expressionless. Ronnie noticed that he didn't have many wrinkles. "No rush."

Smiling, Ronnie took another bite of her avocado toast, thankfully still unfazed by what Pat said it looked like when he first saw it.

After they both finished eating, Ronnie cleared their plates and announced that she had to go to the store that day.

"Again?"

"Fresh produce only lasts so long." Ronnie shrugged. "I try not to buy too much at a time so it won't spoil."

"Umph."

"You doing anything special today?"

"Got some errands to run."

Leaning against the counter, Ronnie looked at Pat curiously. "You like being retired, Dad?"

"Yeah."

"You don't get bored?"

"Nah. I keep myself occupied just fine."

"I'd get restless with nothing to do and nowhere to go."

"Didn't you used to be a housewife?"

"Yeah...but then I was tending to the house and taking care of my husband. That was my job."

"I guess."

"Edward worked to take care of me, so I tried to make sure he didn't have to worry about anything when he got home."

"How come y'all never had any kids?"

There it was. Ronnie had hoped this question wouldn't come up but she figured it was only a matter of time.

"I...just wasn't quite ready for kids yet," she finally answered. She twirled her foot around in a circle and eyed it as she did so.

"Was he?"

"Yes. He, um, he wanted to start a year or so after we got married. But I just kept asking him to wait."

"And he got tired of waitin'?"

This conversation was making Ronnie uncomfortable. She rubbed her arm. "That wasn't the reason we split up."

"Why *did* you split up, then?"

"I'd rather not talk about it, Dad."

"Fine." Pat threw up a hand and took another sip of his coffee.

Her mood shot, Ronnie quickly washed the breakfast dishes and retreated to her room, trying to put the conversation out of her mind. She wasn't yet to the point where she could think about her failed marriage without becoming incredibly sad. And the fact that she never had kids was kind of a sore spot, because it had always been one between her and Edward. He made it clear when they started dating that he wanted to be a father, and Ronnie led him to believe she was all for having as many babies as he wanted. Once they were married, though, she kept putting the brakes on procreation, giving one excuse after another as to why. Edward grew frustrated, but Ronnie thought he would get over it; it wasn't like she *never* wanted to have children. But she apparently underestimated how big of a deal it was to him. Ronnie was sure that her foot-dragging about having children was part of the reason for him leaving her.

Donning a hat and shades, Ronnie went back to Walmart for her groceries. She was still embarrassed from when her card was declined on the last visit, even though there was only one person that knew about that, and the chances of running into the random guy that tried to hit on her was slim. Still, Ronnie was quick as she got her groceries, list and coupons in hand, zipping up and down the aisles before zooming right to self check-out.

Ronnie drove home, deep in thought. Things were slowly starting to look up in her life; she had a nice job working with people she liked, and she and Pat were no longer at each other's throats. Even though she hadn't cared for the subject, it was nice to have an actual conversation with her father. They never talked, they just argued, if they communicated at all. But it looked like things were starting to turn the corner. She knew they had a long way to go, but at least they were headed in the right direction.

When she got home, she went to put her groceries away and noticed that Pat had made some room for her in the refrigerator. Her smile was automatic. It was such a small thing, but she was touched by it. Pat was finally making room for her.

Since he was still out running his errands, Ronnie wanted to do something nice to surprise him for when he got home. When she was done with the groceries, she decided to do all the laundry in the house. She didn't know if Pat had a certain way or routine of doing that, but she figured he would appreciate the gesture, regardless. She quickly gathered her dirty clothes, then everything in his hamper. Pausing at the door of his bedroom, she decided to wash his bedsheets for good measure. She yanked all of the sheets off the bed, including the pillowcases, in too much of a rush to notice that one of them was actually Missy's old nightgown. She just dumped everything into the basket and hurried towards the washing machine, hoping to be done by the time he got back.

She couldn't wait to see his reaction to all of this.

Pat silenced his phone with an annoyed grunt. Debra was calling again. She had left him several messages since they shared a kiss at her home after church, and Pat wasn't ready to talk to her yet. He was still ashamed for letting it happen, and for enjoying it. It had been almost two weeks, and Pat even skipped church because he didn't want to run into her.

When her calls started becoming more frequent, and Pat listened to one of her voicemails that was urgently asking him to call her back, he got a weird feeling in his gut. Something told him this had nothing to do with their kiss. He parked his truck in a nearby parking lot and returned her call.

"Pat, thank goodness," Debra breathed, answering on the first ring.

"What's the matter?"

"Missy is dead."

Pat was glad he had parked, because he would have surely crashed. It took several moments for her words to even register, and when they did, it felt like all the weight had just been punched out of him.

"What you say?" he finally asked, his voice low.

"Missy passed away, Pat. This morning."

Pat couldn't bring himself to speak. He just looked ahead of him, mindlessly noting a man pulling his trashcan to the curb.

"I got a call," Debra began, sensing his shock. "It was from a number in Arizona. Apparently, that's where she's been all this time. The man explained that she showed up there many years ago, claiming she needed to 'find herself.' She was only going to stay for a week or so, but ended up not wanting to leave. It sounded like some kind of shelter or cult or something."

"What?"

"I know, it sounded crazy to me, too. But apparently she told them all about us; me, you, and Ronnie. He was very apologetic that she stayed away so long; apparently, several people tried to get her to at least call us and let us know she was okay, but she opted to just send the postcards. He thought that maybe she was ashamed, and couldn't bring herself to speak to either of us."

So many questions were piling up in Pat's mind, but the same three words blared over all of them: Missy is dead.

"She had a massive stroke last night and didn't wake up this morning. Apparently, she had left instructions to contact us should anything happen to her. As for why she really left in the first place," Debra sniffled, obviously still crying, "We'll probably never know."

Pat just knew this was all a dream that he was going to wake up from any minute. None of this made any sense.

"I, um," he finally croaked. He cleared his throat. "Don't know what to say right now."

"I totally understand. I thought I was being pranked when I got the call this morning, but everything the man told me made sense. He's sending her things and her death certificate. Apparently, she requested to be cremated, so they'll be sending her ashes, too."

His head swimming, Pat put his truck in gear and sped out of the parking lot. At some point, he hung up on Debra without saying goodbye. He couldn't think straight.

Thankfully, he made it to the closest bar he could find in one piece. He didn't want to go home yet in case Ronnie was there; there was no way he could tell her any of this yet when he didn't know how to process it himself. Part of him was still waiting to wake up.

He ordered one beer, then another. Anger and sadness were vying for position like two post players on a basketball court. All these years, he held out hope that Missy would come back. That she would do whatever it was she left to do, and finally get back to her family. Pat felt that if he saw her face again, he would be able to forgive her leaving. All he wanted was his wife back. That's all he ever wanted these past twenty years.

But now, he was never going to get that. The only way he'd get to look into Missy's face would be in pictures. He had no idea what she even looked like before she died; how much she had aged, if she changed her hair, gained some eight, anything. He knew nothing because all she sent was some vague postcards. And he couldn't bring himself to be grateful that she at least sent those. He was angry that she left in the first place.

As angry as he was, though, he was still devastated. Missy had been his first and only; all he knew was her. They fell in love as teenagers and got married as soon as their parents allowed them to. He loved her more than he ever loved anything, working for over thirty years in a shutter factory so she wouldn't have to work. It was that love that sustained him after she left, because he believed she loved him, too. Even when the years started piling up, he held on to the belief that he would see his beloved Missy again. To keep his sanity, he oftentimes acted like she had never left; cooking enough for two, laying out her clothes, talking to an empty room as if she could hear him. It helped him cope with her being gone, even if he seemed nuts doing it. Now he didn't even have that anymore.

Knowing he still had to drive home, Pat stopped after two beers, though he took his time leaving the bar. He parked it in a corner booth and watched a baseball game on one of the small televisions scattered around. Slumped against the wall, he wondered how this day could have taken such a turn for the worst. Earlier he was feeling pretty good about how things were going with Ronnie; they were starting to get along and could be in the same room without fussing. But now, the budding relationship with his daughter was the furthest thing from his mind. He just lost the person who meant the most to him, and the more that it set in that he would never see or speak to Missy again, the more he wanted to break down into a million pieces.

"Can I get you something, sir?" a waitress asked him.

"Just bring me some wings." Pat didn't even look at her.

"Ten? Twenty? And what flavor?"

"I don't care."

Giving him a concerned look, the waitress walked off. Pat didn't even know how much time had passed before she slid a basket of hot lemon pepper wings in front of him, and a cup of water. He eventually pushed off the wall and grabbed a wing, putting the whole thing in his mouth and sliding the meat off the bone with his teeth. It was the first non-home cooked meal he had in years.

When the last wing had been devoured, he tossed some money on the table and trudged back out to his truck. Even though he had just eaten, he still felt empty. The sky was dark now, leaving him to wonder just how long he had been in the bar. Letting out a large belch, he pulled out of the parking lot and headed home.

Ronnie's Pilot was in the driveway. He knew he had to tell her the news, though he had no idea how he was going to do it. Emotional scenes were never his thing, and sensitivity wasn't high on his list of attributes. He didn't even know how Ronnie felt about Missy after all this time. Was she angry? Resentful? Still wishing she would come back? Pat had no idea, because he never asked. But he knew that he had to find some way to tell her; Missy was her mother, after all.

When Pat entered the house, everything was dark. The air smelled fresh, like a flowery fabric softener. He eased towards the hallway and didn't hear anything from Ronnie's room, so he figured she was asleep already. He hated to wake her up, but now that he convinced himself to tell her about Missy, he just wanted to get it over with.

He started to ease her door open, but chickened out and hurried to his own room, closing the door. All he needed was a few minutes to gather himself. Sitting down on the bed, he hung his head, gripping the comforter with both hands and rocking back and forth. His eyes were squeezed shut. A pain he hadn't felt before started to overtake him, as the weight of reality started to set in.

His wife was gone. Dead. Twenty years of waiting for nothing.

Tears began to wet his eyes, but he shook his head vigorously as if to stop them. Pat never liked to cry. Even when his parents died, he did his best to keep the tears from falling. Showing that kind of emotion made him too vulnerable, in his mind. He had to be the rock, no matter what.

Several moments passed before his eyes eased open. He looked down at his hands that were gripping the comforter. A frown bent his brow. This wasn't the way he put his bedsheets on. His comforter was on sideways. There was no way he did that; he was a creature of habit, after all. He made his bed the exact same way every day, and this wasn't the way he left it that morning.

It was then that he smelled the flowers. Leaning down, he sniffed the sheets. Did Ronnie do his laundry? He stood up to check the hamper in his bathroom, and it was empty. Realization caused him to hurry back to his bed and check the pillows. Sure enough, Missy's nightgown wasn't wrapped around the other pillow like it usually was. Ronnie must have washed it and put it away somewhere.

Pat's anger wouldn't let him stop and consider that Ronnie had just been trying to something nice. He was outraged that she came into his room and bothered his things. Namely, Missy's things.

He stormed to the kitchen and yanked open the refrigerator, dumping all of Ronnie's healthy food into the trash in a blind rage. Tears clouded his vision, and a lot of things ended up on the floor, but he didn't care. Whatever was on the floor, he pulverized with his size-twelve boots. All of the anger about Debra and Missy, and himself, had overtaken him.

When all of Ronnie's groceries were destroyed, he was still seething with anger. He stomped towards Ronnie's room, leaving footprints of mashed produce along the way. Part of his mind warned him to calm down before waking his daughter, but he ignored the warning, slamming through the door.

"Ronnie!"

He reached out to shake her arm. As soon as his hand touched her, she jumped, screaming so loudly Pat stepped back.

"Don't touch me!" she yelled, scooting away.

"What you hollerin' for? I got somethin'-"

"No, you don't have anything for me! That's what you always say; *I have something for you.* Well I don't want it!"

"What in the world are you talkin' 'bout??"

"Stay away from me!!" She gathered the sheets in front of her, curling against the wall.

Pat was bewildered, some of his earlier anger dissipating. He had never seen Ronnie freak out like this. Her eyes weren't even open.

"Look here, calm down-"

"Don't tell me to calm down! You can't keep doing this to me! I don't care what you say, I'm telling Mommy! I'll even tell Daddy, even though you said he'd never believe me over you. I'm telling anyway!!"

It was then that Pat realized that she thought he was somebody else. Not sure how to handle it, he tentatively reached out to her, then thought better of it. Her words didn't seem like they were just the result of a bad dream, like he initially thought. She looked absolutely horrified, yet still angry.

"If you touch me again, I'll kill you," Ronnie murmured, her fists clenched against her bent knees. "I'll get a knife and stab you right in the chest. You're lucky I don't keep a knife under my pillow anymore."

Her words caused sent a chill through Pat, cooling off any anger he had left. He inched closer to the bed, his heart thumping hard enough to be heard.

"Ronnie," he hedged cautiously, eyeing her. Tears were flowing freely, but her teeth were gritted in anger, chest heaving rapidly. She was now looking directly at him and he hoped that all she needed was a few moments to recognize him and snap out of whatever this was.

"Stay back!"

"Ronnie, it's me. It's your daddy. I know we never got along all that well, but you know I ain't never put my hands on you."

"Shut up! Stop lying!" Ronnie was screaming at the top of her lungs, hitting the bed with her fists. "Stop lying!"

"I haven't! I never did nothin' to you!"

"Yes you did! And you're *not* my daddy! Don't try to trick me!! Just because y'all are twin brothers doesn't mean you can fool me!"

As if someone pushed him, Pat reeled backwards. She thought he was Alvin?

Before he could say anything or process what was quickly starting to make sense, Ronnie scrambled past him, out of the room, and out of the house, grabbing her purse and keys from the desk.

Realization washed over Pat like a crushing wave. Now Ronnie's animosity towards Alvin made sense. Her confusing him for his identical twin brother when he came into her room in the middle of the night made sense. But when he thought about what she said, and recalled the fear and anger she had in her eyes when she thought he was Alvin, he clutched his chest as reality set in. It didn't take much to put two and two together.

His brother had molested his daughter.

Remembering all the times he had taken Ronnie to Alvin's, all because he didn't want to be bothered with her, caused a pain almost as strong as the one he felt upon hearing of Missy's death. How many times had this happened?

And all because of him.

Sinking to the floor, Pat cried as hard as he ever had in his life.

Chapter 11

Not knowing where else to go, Ronnie ended up at Tess's.
"I didn't know where else to go," she muttered,
looking at her bare feet. She hadn't even put shoes on before
she left Pat's house.

"I'm glad you called me; you're more than welcome here,"
Tess assured her. She sat a cup of steaming chamomile tea on
the end table next to Ronnie before taking a seat in the nearby
armchair. She looked at Ronnie, her eyes soft and empathetic.
"I'm just glad you got here in one piece, as hysterical as you
were when you called."

"I'm sorry about that."

"Stop apologizing."

"I suppose I should tell you what's going on; why I'm here."

"Only if you want to."

"I need to get this stuff off my chest finally."

"Then I'm all ears."

"Well..." Ronnie twisted the damp handkerchief Tess had
given her. "I could tell when I was a little girl that my dad didn't
really like me all that much..."

Ronnie told Tess about her strained relationship with Pat,
and how they grew even further apart after Missy left when
Ronnie was fifteen; how her Uncle Alvin started molesting her
when she was six years old; her failed marriage to Edward and
realizing her own issues with affection; how she had a hard
time letting anyone get close to her, or trusting anyone. The
more she talked, the more she wanted to tell. These were things
she never told anyone about, hadn't even written them in a

diary or journal. Tess became the first person she really opened herself up to; even Edward didn't know about some of these things.

When Ronnie finally stopped talking, spent and emotionally exhausted, Tess wordlessly moved next to her on the couch and wrapped her in her arms. Ronnie automatically stiffened at first, but it only took seconds before she melted into Tess's soft bosom. She cried quietly into Tess's shoulder, appreciating the comfort she didn't even realize she needed.

"Just let it all out, baby," Tess encouraged softly, stroking Ronnie's braids tenderly. "This is good for you. Let it all out."

Ronnie did. She cried for what seemed like hours. Without even realizing when, she began clinging to Tess, growing so attached to her warmth and acceptance that she didn't want to let it go.

After a while, Ronnie dozed off. When she awoke with a start, she glanced at the clock on Tess's television stand and realized a couple of hours had passed. She looked up at Tess, whose head was leaning against the back of the couch. Her eyes were closed. Ronnie noted her turban-wrapped head, thick false eyelashes, and plump lips; things she never paid any attention to before. Small details were things she tended to gloss over about people.

Tess lifted her head and looked at Ronnie. "Hey," she yawned.

"Hey." Ronnie moved her braids from her face. "I should probably go..."

"Girl, stop. It's too late for you to be driving back there tonight. Besides, I doubt you're ready to face your dad yet."

"I can't argue with you there."

"Just stay here tonight. The couch is all yours; it folds out. Deal with everything tomorrow."

Ronnie smiled gratefully. "Thanks, Tess. I appreciate it."

"Don't mention it. I'll get you some blankets."

"Okay."

"And if you want, I'll call your dad for you; let him know where you are."

Part of Ronnie didn't care if Pat knew where she was or not. But she made herself agree. "All right."

After Tess helped Ronnie make up the sofa bed, it didn't take long at all for Ronnie to fall into a deep sleep. It was the first time in a while that she felt safe.

The next morning, Ronnie rubbed her eyes and sat up. It took a few moments to remember where she was. She noticed the cup of cold, untouched tea from the night before. Had the room always smelled like lemongrass?

When she glanced at the clock, she was surprised to see it was almost ten o'clock in the morning.

"Gosh, what day is it?" she muttered, rubbing her eyes.

"Good morning!" Tess greeted brightly, entering the room. Her huge afro was pulled into a puff, and she was wearing a shiny tank top that looked like it was barely containing her huge breasts. Ronnie quickly averted her eyes.

"Morning," she mumbled.

"You hungry? Want some breakfast?"

"Oh, uh, no thanks."

"You sure? You should eat something."

Ronnie recalled how she told Tess so much stuff the night before, and she felt the embarrassment begin to creep over her.

What had she been thinking, spilling her guts to Tess like that? She couldn't even look at her.

"I don't have an appetite." She began looking around for her shoes, temporarily forgetting she hadn't worn any. "I'll just get out of your hair..."

"Oh, I get it," Tess said knowingly. "Starting to regret telling me all your business, huh?"

Ronnie started to deny it, then decided there was no point. "I'm just not used to...*opening up* like that. After what happened with Dad, I wasn't in my usual frame of mind."

"Maybe that's a good thing." Tess rested a knee on the arm of the couch. "Maybe you needed something to shake things up for you. Can you say you were happy with the way your life has been, overall?"

"I...it could be better, I guess. But whose couldn't?"

"Ronnie, look." Tess's face was serious. "You told me some pretty major, heavy stuff last night that, straight up, I'm still kinda reeling from, myself. I had no *idea* that you were dealing with all of that. You're handling it as well as anyone could expect, I guess, but at some point, you're going to need to start dealing with your issues. 'Cause, baby, you *have* some issues. And keeping them to yourself clearly isn't the way to deal with them."

"I guess I figured nobody would care," Ronnie admitted, looking at the floor.

"I don't know your dad. But do you honestly think he wouldn't have cared *at all* if he knew that his brother was molesting you every time he took you to his house?"

Ronnie wanted to say Pat wouldn't have cared. But she knew better than that. She and Pat may have never been close, but she never thought he didn't love her *at all*. That realization just occurred to her.

"Yeah. He would've. And I *know* my mother would have."

"So why didn't you tell anyone back then?" Tess's voice was gentle.

Slowly shaking her head, Ronnie searched for a response that made sense. "Honestly, Tess...I really couldn't tell you. Maybe I felt like I deserved it? After a while, I...just got used to it."

"Wow." Tess looked pained. "No child should have to get used to that."

"It happened so many times. And Uncle Alvin always insisted that his brother would never believe me over him. Told me that Dad didn't even like me; why else would he always take me over there? He made it seem like it was something that was...meant to be."

Tess was now crying. Ronnie wasn't.

"That's horrible. I am so, so sorry that you had to go through that."

Ronnie shrugged. "Thanks."

Several quiet moments passed before Tess slapped her hands against her thighs.

"Well, I need some food," she said loudly, wiping her eyes with her fingertips. "If you still don't wanna eat anything, at least come in the kitchen and keep me company while I eat."

Ronnie dutifully followed her. She wryly thought how Tess and Pat might get along as she watched Tess pull out Texas toast, bacon, and potatoes.

"So...what's on the menu?" Ronnie politely asked.

"Cinnamon French toast, home fries and bacon." Tess's head was still in the refrigerator.

"You really shouldn't eat white bread," Ronnie automatically said. It was like she was on autopilot. "Not to mention coating it in eggs and milk; you'd be surprised how much better you'd feel if you cut back on the dairy. And don't even get me started on the bacon-"

"Ronnie."

"Yeah?"

"Don't try to tell me what to eat."

Ronnie blinked, surprised. "I'm not trying to be offensive. I was just trying to help."

"Who said I needed your help?"

"I...well, just by what you're eating. You have to know it isn't good for you. And then when you couple that with lack of exercise..."

"So you just assume 'cause I'm not a size six that I just sit on my ass, right? You feel it's your job to lecture me on the evils of bread and dairy and bacon, and probably any other kind of meat, because you feel like you have to have control over something."

"What? No! This has nothing to do with control, Tess."

"I think it does. With everything that's gone on in your life that you couldn't do anything about, you have to have the upper hand in *something*. Being a vegan is just another way for you to get to distance yourself from people while still judging them."

"Wow," Ronnie shook her head, reeling. "Barely ten hours later and already using what I told you against me, huh? And I'm more vegetarian than vegan."

"I'm not trying to use anything against you," Tess quickly clarified. She stopped whisking the custard mixture for the French toast and turned to Ronnie, a hand on her hip. "I'm just being straight up. I am not a small woman; never have been. Do you think you're the first person to try to tell me what I should and shouldn't eat?"

"I'm guessing I'm not."

"No, you're not. But little did they know and little do *you* know, most of the time, I eat healthy. Green smoothies, lots of fruits and vegetables, mostly seafood, and I chug water like it's going out of business. *And* I work out four or five days out of the week. But I don't obsess over calories or act like sweets and meat are the devil. If I want to indulge, I do. Life is just too short to be hung up on that."

For the first time, Ronnie took a real look at Tess. All she ever really noticed were her huge breasts, but she actually had an hourglass shape. It was just a large hourglass. Starting to feel a little silly, Ronnie bit her lip.

"I apologize. I guess I jumped to conclusions."

"Yeah, you did." Tess resumed cooking.

Taking a seat at the small kitchen table, Ronnie thought about Tess's earlier accusation. She never considered her vegetarianism as something that made her superior over anyone or as a platform for judgment, but the more she thought about it, the more she could see how Tess came to that. When she became a vegetarian in college, it drove her roommates crazy how she would always comment on their five dollar pepperoni pizzas, or try to get them to switch to sorbet when they would have ice cream on Friday nights. Edward was certainly no fan of never having real meat in the house; they had constant arguments about that. And Pat accused her of trying to control him more than once, when it came to food.

Ronnie frowned as all of these realizations hit her. When she became a vegetarian, it was a way to make her feel better. She was still distraught over Missy being gone, she had spent many nights drowning her sorrows in chicken wings and pasta, and just wanted to take control of her life in some way. If she couldn't feel good emotionally, she could at least look good. But she didn't realize how she was lording her own principles over the people around her.

Tess was softly humming to herself as she cooked. It sounded like some kind of gospel tune. Ronnie glanced over at her as she seasoned her home fries and flipped the French toast, as the bacon sizzled in the background. Ronnie would be lying if she said the aromas weren't at least a little enticing. She used to live on that kind of stuff and suddenly remembered how much she used to love it. Her stomach growled and she hoped Tess couldn't hear it.

Finally, Tess joined her at the table, plate piled high. Ronnie felt herself eyeing it, not out of disdain as she had taught herself to do over the years with such food, but actually out of yearning.

My head must still be messed up from last night, she justified to herself.

Several quiet moments passed, with Tess eating her breakfast and Ronnie watching her do so.

"Tess, I sincerely apologize for crossing a line earlier," Ronnie finally said. "I guess I never realized the attitude I have when it comes to food."

Swallowing a bite of French toast, Tess winked at her. "Apology accepted."

"You're certainly not the first person I've ticked off about this stuff. But you're the first one to make me realize *I* might be the problem."

"I think you were just ready to hear it now. Sometimes things have to happen before we're ready to accept some things about ourselves."

"True." Ronnie smiled. "Were you this wise in high school?"

"Oh girl, no." Tess chuckled, wiping some errant syrup from her hand with a napkin. "I was a mess in high school. Let's just say life has taught me well."

Ronnie was curious as to exactly what Tess had gone through in the years they were out of touch, but felt too nervous to ask, even though she had bared her own soul the night before. And Tess certainly wasn't the shy type.

"I'll probably tell you all about it one day," Tess continued, as if reading Ronnie's mind. "But I think we've both had enough heavy stuff for a little while."

"You're right about that." Ronnie's eyes strayed to Tess's plate again.

Noticing, Tess cut off a corner of her French toast and a small piece of bacon, and slid her plate closer to Ronnie.

Only hesitating for a second, Ronnie took the small morsels of food and popped them into her mouth. Her eyes slid closed. She hadn't had bacon, *real* bacon, in years and she remembered why she used to love whenever Missy or Pat made it on Saturday and Sunday mornings. In that moment, she didn't care about sodium or nitrates or any of that. It was just damn good.

"Yum," she whispered without realizing it.

Tess grinned. "Girl...you're gonna be all right."

Chapter 12

It was later on in the day when Ronnie finally went back to Pat's. She didn't know what she was going to say to her father about what happened the night before. She didn't even know if Pat would want to talk about it. It wasn't like he tried to call her after she ran out of the house into the night, crying and barefoot.

The house was quiet and dark. Ronnie knew Pat was home because his truck was outside, so she headed straight for his bedroom. She gently knocked on the door, then listened for movement. Hearing none, she knocked again.

"Dad?" she called out.

No response. She tried to turn the knob, but it was locked. Figuring he was asleep, Ronnie figured she'd just talk to him later. Thankful for the reprieve, she went into her own room and locked the door.

Pat had heard Ronnie, but ignored her. He was curled up on his bed, surrounded by Missy's things; clothes, empty perfume bottles, books, pictures, and anything else he could find in his room.

"I'm sorry," he muttered. "I'm so sorry."

He was apologizing for what he learned happened to his daughter. For not being a better father. Evidently not being a good enough husband. And for giving up hope on Missy.

It ate at him that after twenty years of waiting and believing that he would see his wife again, he kissed another woman. Another woman who happened to be his sister-in-law. He wondered if this had been a year or even a couple of months earlier, if he would have even accepted Debra's dinner invitation. The only thing he missed the previous twenty years had been Missy; he never really yearned for other female attention. But as soon as his strength started to slip, Missy dies. He felt like he let her down, and he would never forgive himself for it.

It was only because his stomach was growling so hard that it hurt that Pat finally left his room. He was surprised to see Ronnie in the living room, having forgotten she had come back.

"Oh...didn't know you were out here," he mumbled. He kept his bloodshot eyes averted.

"You've been crying." Ronnie didn't bother asking because it was clear he had been. And she knew he wouldn't admit it, anyway.

Clearing his throat, Pat took a couple of steps towards the kitchen before stopping suddenly, turning back to his daughter.

"Alvin molested you?"

Ronnie put down the book she hadn't been able to concentrate on. "Yes. He did."

"A lot?"

"Since I was six."

Wincing, Pat took a seat on the other end of the couch. He slowly rubbed his calloused hands together. "'Round the age I started insistin' on takin' you over there."

"Yes."

"Do you wanna talk 'bout this? With me?"

"I actually do."

"I'm listenin.'"

"Well," Ronnie sat forward, trying to gather her words. "The first couple of times I went over there were okay. He was really nice, letting me watch cartoons and feeding me ice cream, playing games with me. I had fun. But then...things started to change after that."

Pat tried to steel himself.

"He would insist that I take a bath as soon as I got there. And he wouldn't let me take it by myself; he had to be in there. Said he knew just what to do with me. That was the first time he touched me...*that way*. I didn't like it but whenever I tried to move away or ask why he was doing that, he just said that I needed to trust him. That he knew what was best for me. That this is what good little girls did with their favorite uncles."

Pat shifted in his seat, clearly uncomfortable. A frown etched his face.

"After a while, I got used to it, even though I never liked it. When I got to be a teenager, he started showing me porn, saying it was time I became a woman. Up until that point, it had been all hand stuff; him touching me and making me touch him. But when I got to be thirteen, I guess he figured it was time to kick things up a notch."

Ronnie paused to take a swig from the water bottle that was on the coffee table next to her. "I remember you and Mama were going to some function at the church; I think it was a revival. Mama wanted me to go with you two; I asked if I could go, too. Almost begged, even though church had never been my favorite place to be. But anything would've been better than going to Uncle Alvin's. But you refused; said I didn't know how to behave at church. Said I'd have a lot more fun at your brother's house."

Remembering the exact day she was talking about, Pat hung his head. He had thought it was a little strange how much Ronnie was begging him and Missy to take her with them, especially considering she never seemed to care about church that much before. But Pat just wanted a night with Missy, without having to worry about looking after Ronnie.

And Alvin always insisted that she was always welcome anytime. It was the perfect solution, as far as Pat was concerned. He had no idea that Alvin was doing such things to his daughter.

"It was called *Sixteen Strokes*," Ronnie recalled. "We ate dinner first. Then he put the movie on, saying we were going to watch it together. I asked if we could watch something else; he said no. He made me sit really close to him on the couch. I didn't even want to look at the screen. Then he started moaning, getting excited by what we were watching. He put my hand on his crotch, then moaned louder. Then he kissed me for the first time, on the mouth. Pushed his tongue into my mouth and touched my breasts. I hated it and asked if we could stop; he said no. That it was time. Then he pulled out the condom."

Shooting up off the couch, Pat jammed his fists into his pockets. "You don't have to say no more."

"Might as well tell you all of it, right?" Ronnie looked at him with glassy eyes. There was a clear edge in her voice. "I had to endure it for years; the least you can do is listen for a few minutes."

Slightly taken aback, Pat swallowed and nodded.

"He took my virginity," Ronnie stated bluntly. "Right there on his living room couch. It hurt, but he said that wouldn't last long; that eventually I'd start liking it. I never did. But it didn't matter. What I wanted never mattered."

Tears were stinging Pat's eyes. He tried like hell to keep them at bay.

"One night I told him I didn't want to do that with him anymore. I threatened to tell you and Mama about it," Ronnie continued. "But he said you would never believe he would do something like that. Said you never liked me; you never wanted a daughter. Told me that you must have wanted me to be with him since you were always leaving me over there. And as far as Mama went, he'd just tell her I was lying. There was no way she'd think someone who worked around kids every day would do such a thing. He'd just say you were making it up to get out of coming to his house, since I'd made it clear that I didn't like going over there. But all of this happened. It really happened."

Ronnie was crying silent tears. It was the first time she really detailed everything that happened during those visits to her Uncle Alvin all those years ago. Ever since then, she tried her best to put it out of her mind. But it no doubt still affected her; it caused lasting issues with affection, which was a big part of the reason Edward chose to end their marriage. That, and the fact that she never told him about any of it. Maybe if he knew the reasoning behind why she was the way she was, he would've been more understanding and patient. Acknowledging that to herself only brought more tears.

"So," Pat cleared his throat. "You never said anything 'cause of what he told you?"

Ronnie looked up, right into his eyes. "Honestly, I believed him, Dad. I didn't think you would care one way or the other."

Sadly, Pat knew there was no way he could question her on that. He knew he hadn't been much of a father to her, outside of providing everything she needed. They weren't close and never had been, because Pat had never been interested in being close. He never got over her being a girl, when he wanted a boy. Of course he loved her, but it was the bare minimum, and he knew it.

"I would've cared," he insisted. "I know it's my fault you believe I wouldn't, but I woulda."

"Did you know about it?" Ronnie was still looking at him. "Did you know about what he used to do to me?"

"No!" The answer was immediate and emphatic, more emphatic than Ronnie had ever heard anything spoken from Pat, outside of when he was fussing at her. "I swear on your mama's name, I never knew nothin' 'bout what Alvin was doin'. None. If I had, I'da surely done somethin' 'bout it. There's no way I woulda let that go on."

"Really?"

"Yes, really. And I pray you believe me on that."

Turning away, Ronnie shook her head. "I don't know what to believe, Dad."

The shame and guilt for what happened to his daughter, and his hand in it, sucked the strength from Pat's legs. He groped for the nearest chair, dropping into it and running his rough hands down his face. He thought he couldn't feel worse after hearing about Missy's passing, but he was wrong. He had never felt as ashamed of himself as he did right then.

"I admit I didn't wanna be bothered with ya," he muttered after a long silence. "I ain't proud of it, but I admit it. But as God as my witness, I had no idea my brother was puttin' his hands on you like that. And knowin' it probably wouldn't have happened if I wasn't always takin' you ova there is hurtin' my soul right now. I'm ashamed of myself. And I know Missy would be, too."

Ronnie looked over at him. His anguish was clear. He was hunched over, seemingly about to fall out of the chair. Ronnie had never seen him look so broken down.

"Please forgive me."

It was a whisper, but Ronnie heard it. She didn't know if he was talking to her or God, but she found herself standing and going over to him. Crouching in front of him, she placed her hands on his arms, the gesture unfamiliar. Pat lifted his head slightly and looked at her, his eyes bloodshot and exhausted from everything he had learned over the past couple of days.

"I'm so sorry," he whispered, looking right into her eyes.

The floodgates opened again, and Ronnie's eyes welled with tears so fast she couldn't have stopped it if she wanted to. She wrapped her arms around Pat's neck, and cried harder when he immediately returned her hug. It was the first one Ronnie could remember getting from him, probably ever.

They cried together for everything they lost, learned, and were starting to gain together.

Chapter 13

Waking up in her bed the next morning, Ronnie wasn't even sure how she ended up there. The last thing she remembered was crying in her father's arms last night, a thought so foreign to her she began to wonder if she dreamt the whole thing.

It had been a whirlwind of emotions the past couple of days, and Ronnie's head was pounding. A glance at the clock reminded her that she had to be at work in a few hours, and she didn't know how she was going to plaster a smile on her face when the last thing she felt like doing was smiling or being around people. But Tess had been too good to her to bail without a good reason, and just not wanting to be at work wasn't an example of that. So she threw the covers off of her and rolled out of bed.

Pat was usually up having is breakfast around this time, but Ronnie didn't smell anything coming from the kitchen. Even though she never knew him to sleep past seven, she peeked into his room just in case the emotional exhaustion from the previous night kept him in bed, but to her surprise, his door was wide open. Even more alarming, his bed wasn't made, which was totally unlike him. Pat was a creature of habit, and always made his bed before going to make his breakfast. And he never left his door wide open like this, whether he was in the room or not.

"Dad?" she called out.

Ronnie frowned. Something wasn't right. She peeked into his bathroom before quickly heading towards the kitchen.

The house was quiet, too quiet. No TV, no banging pots, no sizzling meats. No humming like Pat usually did when he cooked, or mumbling to himself as he ate. Dread coursed through Ronnie like a run in some pantyhose.

"Dad!"

When she rushed into the kitchen, Pat was sitting at the table with a large mug and a bottle of pills in front of him. There was no food anywhere. Pat was just staring into the mug, as if he was trying to work up the nerve to drink the contents.

Concerned, Ronnie went and sat next to him at the table, looking at him.

"What's wrong?"

It was then that she smelled the bleach. She glanced around the room and didn't get the sense that it had just been cleaned, and her eyes landed on the cup. Leaning closer, she could tell it was bleach that Pat was staring into.

"Oh my god!" she exclaimed, moving the cup away as carefully as she could without sloshing it, since it was filled almost to the rim. She snatched the bottle of pills, noticing it was an old Percocet prescription of his from two years ago. She looked angrily at her father, who still hadn't acknowledged her presence. "Where you going to actually try to kill yourself??"

Pat's eyes never moved. "Might as well."

"Might as well? Why in the world would you say something like that? Just because of what I told you about Uncle Alvin last night? As bad as that is, it's not worth killing yourself over, Dad! I know you're feeling guilty but this is just taking the easy way out, as far as I'm concerned!"

"Yo' mama's gone..."

"What? Dad, Mama's been gone for twenty years! You never wanted to kill yourself because of it before now!"

It was then that Pat remembered that Ronnie still didn't know about Missy passing. She freaked out and ran out of the house, thinking he was Alvin, before he could tell her the other night. Pat hung his head for a moment before looking at his daughter.

"You still don't know."

"Know what?"

Pat didn't want to just blurt it out, but he didn't have the energy to sugarcoat. "Missy died."

Gasping, Ronnie leaned back. "Wh-what? When?"

"A few days ago. It's hard to remember the exact day now. Debra called and told me."

Her hand on her chest, Ronnie plunked against the back of the chair. The news saddened her, but she wasn't devastated. Missy had been gone twenty years; Ronnie spent many nights crying and grieving, not knowing if she was dead or alive. Pat never showed her any of the postcards from Missy over the years confirming she was okay, so as far as Ronnie was concerned, Missy had died years ago.

"I waited twenty years," Pat marveled. He was looking straight ahead. "*Twenty years*. All that time, and I never even got to say goodbye."

"Dad," Ronnie tentatively placed a hand on his arm. She still didn't feel totally comfortable touching him. "I know you're hurting. You loved Mama, probably more than you loved anyone. But please don't make things worse by hurting yourself. You're still here; you have plenty of life left to live."

Pat grunted and looked away.

"Don't forget, I lost her, too," Ronnie reminded him. "Close or not, I don't want to lose two parents in a week. Let's be here for each other." Her grip tightened on his arm. "The way we used to be doesn't have to be the way we are from here on out. We can change things if we want to."

After several thoughtful moments, Pat nodded, clamping his hand over hers.

Ronnie still didn't want to go to work, but she figured the distraction would do her good. And to Pat's chagrin, she dragged him along with her.

"I don't need no babysitter," he grumbled from the passenger seat her of Pilot.

"Well, when I catch my dad about to down a bottle of pills and chase it with bleach, I don't consider him a good candidate for being by himself."

"I lost my head for a minute but I'm not gon' do nothin' crazy."

"I don't believe you, Dad. So I'm afraid you'll just have to indulge me."

"And just what in the world am I supposed to do sittin' in a hair salon? I hope we ain't gon' be there all day."

"It's my job, Dad. I work all day."

"Well, I'm gon' have to call me a taxi or somethin'."

"Hardly anybody uses taxis nowadays, Dad. They use Uber."

"What the heck is that?"

Ronnie couldn't help but chuckle. She was enjoying having Pat with her, despite his surly attitude. Given everything that happened in the previous few days, she wouldn't expect him to be any other way. No one that just lost their wife and learned their twin brother had molested their daughter would be walking on air.

When they arrived at Fierce and 'Fro, Ronnie turned to Pat. "I promise I'll try to get us out of here as soon as possible, okay? I'm sure Tess will understand, given the circumstances."

Pat's eyes snapped to her. "She knows 'bout all this?"

"She doesn't know everything but she knows enough. It was her house I ran to the other night. She called you, remember?"

"Oh. I guess."

When they entered the salon, Tess greeted them immediately.

"Hey, girl," she said, giving Ronnie a hug. She smiled at Pat. "Hey, Mr. Duncan. I'm Tess. It's good to match a face with the name, finally."

Pat took her offered hand, though not quite meeting her eyes. "Nice to meet ya."

"I didn't want to leave him home by himself," Ronnie explained, looking at Tess pointedly.

"No problem at all. He's more than welcome."

"I'll just sit over here in the corner or somethin' where I'm outta the way." Pat's eyes were still averted.

"Nonsense. You're at home here. You want something to drink? We've got some hot coffee and croissants in the back."

Pat's ears perked up, and Ronnie almost laughed. She figured he hadn't eaten anything yet.

"You got jelly?" Pat asked.

"Oh, we got grape jelly, strawberry jelly, apple jelly, butter, a toaster..."

''Nuff said." Pat finally looked at Tess, his eyes widening slightly when they landed on her huge breasts before quickly scooting up to her face. Ronnie had to turn her face away to hide her laugh. Even Tess looked amused.

"You just come on with me, sir," Tess hooked her arm through Pat's. To Ronnie's surprise, Pat didn't look put off by it at all. He wasn't considered the warmest person around strangers, but he seemed to take to Tess immediately. Then again, it was hard not to like Tess. "Ronnie, your daddy is just the cutest thing!"

If Ronnie didn't know better, Pat was actually blushing a little bit. She chuckled. "I suppose."

While Tess tended to Pat, Ronnie proceeded with preparing for the work day. She was glad she brought Pat with her, and not only so she could keep an eye on him. Getting out of the house and meeting some new people would do him good, and it seemed like it already was. She didn't expect him to forget about everything that happened, but she at least hoped that he would realize there was more good in his life than bad, regardless of how bleak it might seem at the time.

The day started as usual, with the rest of the staff coming in. They all fussed and fawned over Pat like he was a newborn baby. Ronnie never thought of her father as adorable, but everyone seemed to think he was exactly that.

Instead of Pat hanging out in the waiting area with a magazine like he expected (and hoped) to do, Tess brought a chair near her station and had him sitting right on the salon floor. At first he was a little uncomfortable being in the midst of so many strangers, but after a while he loosened up somewhat. He wasn't talking much but whenever someone asked him a question, it didn't bother him to answer it. It seemed being out of his house and around all of the memories of Missy was doing him some good, if only temporarily.

"Do you want some more coffee, Mr. Duncan?" Tameka asked him.

"I'm all right, thank ya."

"I can get you another muffin," Raja offered.

"I already had two of 'em. Y'all tryin' to make me big as a house," Pat chuckled.

Ronnie thought this was an ironic statement from him, considering how he didn't seem to mind eating calorie-laden meals the rest of the time. But she kept her mouth shut.

"I told y'all you don't have to make a fuss over me," Pat continued. "I 'preciate the kindness but just do yo' work like you usually would. I know where it is if I want some more."

"My daddy isn't here anymore so it's nice to have someone to cater to like I used to cater to him," Raja commented, a wistful smile on her face. "I was a total daddy's girl. Spoiled him rotten. It did kinda get on his nerves sometimes, though, 'cause he said I wouldn't leave him alone."

"Mine, too," Rhoda agreed. "Whenever he was leaving the house, I was bugging him about where he was going, especially when he started getting up in age. Drove him crazy but he knew it was only because I loved him so much."

"I never even *knew* my daddy," Tess commented as she effortlessly parted her client's hair down the middle in a line that would've taken Ronnie several attempts to get as straight. "He abandoned my mama at the hospital when she was in labor with me. Guess it got too real for him and he freaked out; said he was going to get her some ice chips and kept going right on out the door."

"Are you serious?" Vanessa marveled. "He really left her while she was in *labor*?"

"He surely did."

"So you don't know who he is?"

"Yeah, I know who he is. When I got a little older, Mama showed me some pictures. Last I heard, he was living in Savannah somewhere. And he can rot there. He's dead to me."

Ronnie's jaw was hung open in shock. She had no idea.

Then, the proverbial light came on. Pat might not have been thrilled at her being a girl when she was born, but at least he stuck around and took care of her. He didn't leave. It was a perspective she never considered until right then.

The more she thought about it, the more anger she actually felt towards her mother. Missy was the one who just up and left one day and never came back. Except for the one call Ronnie missed a few years back, Missy never tried to keep in touch with her or check in. Not even to let her know she was still alive. What kind of person just left their only child like that? Twenty years without a letter, call or a visit? Ronnie had always revered her mother, all of the fond memories from her childhood painting a rosy picture for Ronnie to lean on in the times when she missed her mother the most. But Missy was out of her life more than she was in it. Pat was the one who stayed.

Their estrangement after Ronnie went to college was mostly Ronnie's doing, not his. She never called and checked on him. She never visited. He could've had an accident or a heart attack, and she never would have known because she was so hell-bent on separating herself from that part of her life. Pat wasn't the best father, and there were plenty of things he could've done better, but she was suddenly realizing that he was the best he could be back then. Ronnie certainly couldn't claim any awards for being a great daughter. In fact, hearing Raja and Rhoda talk about how they cared so much for their fathers made Ronnie realize just how big of a hand she played in everything.

It wasn't all on Pat. Maybe most of it was, but not all of it.

And at the end of the day, he stayed. Helped put her through college, even though they weren't communicating. Let her come back home when Edward put her out, rent-free and with no timetable. Missy was nowhere to be found.

Ronnie looked over at Pat with a newfound appreciation. Their relationship was far from perfect or ideal and still needed a ton of work, but she felt immensely thankful for the fact that he was even there. At one of the lowest times of her life, he was there for her. Tears welled in her eyes.

Tameka noticed. "Ronnie, what's wrong?"

Ronnie slowly walked over to where Pat was sitting and put a hand on his shoulder. She made no move to wipe her tears or pretend like nothing was wrong. Pat looked up at her curiously.

"My mother died," Ronnie said flatly. Several people around her gasped. "And she had been gone out of my life for twenty years; I haven't seen or spoken to her since I was fifteen years old. No clue where she went or why she went there. And hearing you all speak so highly of your fathers, and hearing how yours left like he did, Tess, just makes me realize how fortunate I am to have my dad here. Even though we never had the closest relationship, when my mother left and my husband left, he was the one that was there for me." She pushed her braids out of her face and smiled, sniffling. "Really, when I was at my lowest point in life, all of the people that have been there for me are right here in this room. And I'm...I'm so truly thankful for all of you."

The whole room was in tears. Even Pat's eyes were glistening. Tess patted her client's shoulder before stepping over and enveloping Ronnie in a warm hug. Vanessa, Raja, Tameka, and Rhoda all quickly followed suit, giving her and Pat a big group hug. Even a couple of the clients joined in.

"We are absolutely here for you, baby," Tess assured her. "I told you, we're all family here. Whatever you need, you just say the word."

"You and Mr. Duncan are *both* family," Raja added. "You've got five sisters now so you can hang up that only child stuff."

"Mr. Duncan, you can handle five more daughters, can't you?" Rhoda asked with a smile.

"Lord, y'all tryin' to kill me," Pat joked. He was smiling, something Ronnie wasn't used to seeing from him, and the sight made her smile. He seemed to really appreciate all of the attention and encouragement. "If I can handle everything I've dealt with this far, I can handle that, I reckon."

"Good!" Rhoda leaned down and hugged his neck.

"And as your sister, Ronnie, I feel it's only right that I offer to do your hair for you," Vanessa chimed in. "'Cause, girl, those braids have overstayed their welcome big-time."

Ronnie started to get offended, but found herself laughing along with everyone else. Loudly. If this is what she missed by being an only child growing up, she was going to enjoy this new phase in her life, even if it did take some getting used to.

"Well, I'm on a budget so I've been trying to get as much wear out of them as I can."

"Trust me, you've gotten it. But don't even worry about it, girl, 'cause I'm gonna hook you up. You can pay me in Krispy Kremes."

"Deal!" Ronnie gave her a high five.

"Hell, can I get that deal?" Vanessa's client joked. Her bushy red hair was halfway braided.

"Sorry, girl. Sisters only." Vanessa winked at Ronnie before ushering her client back to the salon chair.

Tess pulled Ronnie aside as everyone resumed their work and conversation.

"If you need some time off, you've got it," she informed her. "Take all the time you need."

"I appreciate it, Tess. And I'll let you know if I do. But being here around you guys has been really good for me. And I see it's been good for Dad, too. I appreciate you letting me bring him today."

"No problem. He's always welcome." She eyed Ronnie. "You sure you're all right?"

"I will be," Ronnie said after a thoughtful moment. "I know I still have a long way to go, but I can honestly say I'm feeling pretty positive. I've never had much of that so it's a nice feeling."

Tess smiled at her, not able to resist giving her another hug. Ronnie gladly received it, feeling as optimistic as she had ever felt.

After they left the salon, Pat strapped himself into Ronnie's car and asked, "You mind if we go by the Wal-Mart before goin' to the house?"

"Sure." Ronnie glanced at him curiously. "What is it you need?"

"Just gotta replace some stuff."

When they arrived at Wal-Mart, Ronnie was surprised to see Pat go right to the produce section.

"You gon' have to let me know what all it is of yours I threw in the trash the other night," Pat said to her. "My memory ain't what it used to be."

Touched, Ronnie placed a hand to her chest. It had certainly been a shock to her when she realized that most of her groceries had been stomped on and trashed.

"That was the night I found out about Missy passing," Pat explained. "Then when I got home, I saw you had washed my clothes. You washed Missy's nightgown that I had wrapped around the pillow on the bed. I'd sprayed the last lil' bit of her perfume on that nightgown; it was the last of all the ones she'd left behind when she left. When I saw you washed it out, I lost my head. It's no excuse, but that's why I threw away your groceries. But I wanna make it right now."

"Oh, dad...I'm so sorry for that. I didn't know."

"I know you didn't. You couldn'ta. You was just tryin' to do somethin' nice."

"I was. But I appreciate you letting me know why you did that; it makes much more sense now. I just thought you were being mean."

"I'm a lot 'a things but I ain't evil. And destroying stuff somebody spent their good money on for no good reason is evil, if ya ask me."

"You're right, you *aren't* evil," Ronnie agreed, looking at her dad in yet another new light. "Difficult, maybe, but not evil."

"I been called worse. Now let's get this rabbit food of yours so I can get back to the house and watch the game."

Shaking her head, Ronnie couldn't help but chuckle as she yanked a produce bag from a nearby roll. "Okay, Dad."

Chapter 14

"We 'bout to have some company," Pat announced a couple of nights later.

Ronnie immediately started to ask if it was Uncle Alvin coming by for dinner and cards again, but figured Pat wouldn't do that after learning of Ronnie's allegations against him. She was still wondering when and if Pat was even going to confront Alvin about it.

"Who?" she asked casually.

"Debra."

"Oh, Aunt Debra?"

"Yep."

"Wow, I haven't seen her in years. She coming for dinner or something?"

"She can eat if she wants to. But she just called and asked if she could stop by. I imagine it's got somethin' to do with Missy."

Pat was preparing ox tails and gravy, blackeyed peas and cornbread. Ronnie convinced him to let her make a fresh salad to go with it, which she considered a small victory.

Debra arrived a short time later and Ronnie was taken aback by just how much she looked like Missy. She mainly only saw her aunt at church and after she left home, Ronnie had stopped going to that church as part of her efforts to separate herself from Pat and memories of her mother.

"Ronnie!" Debra exclaimed happily. She held her arms out. "I haven't seen you in too long. You've grown to be such a beautiful young woman!"

"Thank you. It's good to see you, Aunt Debra."

"It's wonderful to see you. I hate that it's been so long. Can I have a hug?"

Ronnie stepped into the aunt's arms and immediately felt herself getting emotional. Her eyes slid closed, inhaling Debra's soft flowery scent. The comfort she found in Debra's warm embrace was so motherly, something she missed over the years. She laid her head on her aunt's shoulder, clinging to her. Debra gladly welcomed the tightened hug, smoothing Ronnie's braids from her face and resting her cheek on the top of her head.

Pat stood by and watched the interaction. She saw how Ronnie clung to Debra, and realized just how much Ronnie must've missed having a mother all these years. He could imagine how hard it must have been for her to get married with her mother not there, and not even able to tell her about it. Ronnie and Missy were always close. Pat knew Debra couldn't take Missy's place, but maybe she could be that female figure in Ronnie's life, if that's what they both wanted.

"So Debra, what brings you by?" Pat asked after several moments.

"Dad." Ronnie lightly admonished, still holding on to Debra. "Let's at least offer her some dinner first."

"Oh, right." He looked at Debra. "You wanna eat?"

Debra and Ronnie laughed. Some things about Pat would never change. "That would be wonderful, Pat, thank you. It sure smells good."

"Come on, then."

"You sure it's not an imposition?"

"Oh, not at all. Dad always makes enough to feed an army."

"Guess I'm still not used to just makin' smaller portions yet." Pat shrugged. Ronnie looked at him worriedly, but he seemed okay. "You're welcome to it. There's plenty."

The three of them headed to the kitchen, each washing their hands in the sink. Debra helped herself to a healthy portion of Pat's meal, but she also got some of the salad Ronnie made. This made Ronnie smile, even though she wasn't sure why.

"This salad is delicious," Debra raved. "What is it dressed with?"

"Just olive oil, lime juice, salt and pepper," Ronnie replied. "Nothing fancy."

"I love it. I always thought there was nothing better than ranch dressing for a salad but you've surely proved me wrong. I'm going to start dressing my salads at home like this."

Ronnie beamed. It was nice to hear someone enjoy what she made; she was still trying to get Pat to even try her cooking. "I'm so glad you like it. It's just as good with lemon, too."

"I can imagine. Why don't you have any salad, Pat?"

Shrugging, Pat took a big bite of his cornbread. "No reason."

"You should try some. It's so fresh and delicious; goes wonderfully with these ox tails."

Pat eyed her. "You like the ox tails?"

"They're the best I've had. And I've had plenty. You might even make them better than I do."

Smiling, Pat ducked his head slightly. Ronnie thought it was kinda cute how he was blushing. He clearly took a lot of pride in his cooking.

Debra put a small serving of salad on a plate and slid it over to Pat with a wink. To Ronnie's surprise, Pat actually pulled the plate closer to him and took a bite. Ronnie eyed him.

"It's not bad," he finally said. He went in for another bite. "I like the tomatoes and onions in it."

Debra winked at Ronnie. Ronnie considered her aunt a miracle worker. Instead of being put off by Pat only trying her "rabbit food" when someone else suggested it, Ronnie realized Debra had a way with Pat that probably few people did, if anyone. And if Pat could step out of his comfort zone a little, so could Ronnie.

"Dad, can you pass the cornbread?"

Pat looked at her, clearly surprised. "What you want it for?"

Ronnie and Debra laughed. "I'd like to have a piece, if that's okay."

"I thought you didn't eat cornbread. It's got eggs and stuff in it, you know. And I cooked it in leftover bacon grease."

"I'm not a vegan, Dad. I eat eggs. And as for the bacon grease, well," Ronnie shrugged. "One piece won't kill me."

Without another word, Pat slid the pan of cornbread over to Ronnie, who cut herself a small piece. He watched her as she took a delicate bite.

"Oh wow," she marveled, nodding her head. "I have to admit that's good. That is really, really good."

Pat smiled, glancing at Debra, who winked at him. He suddenly remembered the kiss they shared at her house and felt his face go hot. He turned his attention to his blackeyed peas.

"So let me tell you two why I wanted to come by tonight," Debra said when they were all done eating. She dabbed her mouth with a paper towel. "We're going to have a small memorial service for Missy this weekend."

"A funeral?" Ronnie asked.

"Not really a funeral. Just a small ceremony to honor her memory. I'd love for you two to come, but if you don't feel like you can, I understand."

"I guess it's only right that we do," Ronnie mused, playing with her fork.

"Please don't feel obligated, baby. I know you must be angry at your mama for leaving the way she did. I certainly am. That's one of the main reasons I started seeing a therapist."

Pat's head snapped up. "You seein' a shrink?"

"I certainly am. My sister went away for reasons I'll probably never know and then died. My fiancé died a week before we were to be married. My parents died with broken hearts because they had no idea where their oldest daughter was. It's a lot to deal with and it's helpful to have someone help me sort through all of that."

"Well, if it works for ya," Pat shrugged dismissively.

"I think you should consider going to therapy too, Pat."

"What?"

"Both of you. There's nothing wrong with getting help."

"It's not a bad idea," Ronnie agreed. "I know I have more than a few issues."

"Black folks don't need therapy," Pat grumbled.

"Oh Pat, please don't tell me you feed into that ignorant stigma," Debra admonished. "That thinking is why so many of our people are suffering unnecessarily now."

"Yeah, Dad, going to therapy is nothing to be ashamed of," Ronnie added. "And besides, it's nobody's business. I really think you should consider it. We can go together."

"If I wanna talk to somebody, I'll call the pastor. I'm not gonna pay good money for some doctor to try to make me blame everything on my mama." Pat crossed his arms defiantly.

"See, now you're just being stubborn."

"Hopefully you'll at least think about it," Debra said, choosing not to continue trying to persuade him. When he had his heels dug in like this, there was no swaying him. "I think it would do you some good."

"Me, too," Ronnie agreed.

Pat just frowned and grunted.

A short time later, Debra left and Pat immediately retreated to his room. He hadn't had much to say after the therapy suggestion, and Ronnie figured it was best to just leave him alone for a while. She wasn't sure why he got so offended by being told he should go to therapy, and unfortunately their minimal relationship to that point left her at a loss when it came to those kinds of insights. She simply didn't know her father very well, when it came down to it.

With a tired sigh, Ronnie proceeded to clean up the kitchen, then went to relax in the living room. She turned on the television but couldn't find anything she wanted to watch, so she turned it off. Her mind replayed her Aunt Debra's visit. Ronnie had been taken aback by how much she reminded her of Missy. Debra was shorter and her body was fuller, but their faces were practically identical. It was a shock to Ronnie after not seeing her aunt for years, and being able to hug and talk to someone so close to her mother affected her. She was a little surprised at how easily she took to Debra; they always got along okay, but they were never close. Ronnie realized there wasn't really anyone she could say she *was* close with coming up, other than Missy. And when Missy left, Ronnie emotionally separated herself from everyone.

Picking up her phone, Ronnie opened the voicemail she refused to delete. Turning the volume all the way up, she replayed the message from Missy, chewing her bottom lip.

"I'll be back soon. Love you, my Ronnie."

Ronnie replayed the message a couple more times before Pat came rushing into the room, looking around frantically.

"Missy? Missy?"

Sitting up, Ronnie watched her father look around for her mother. She'd never seen him so frantic.

"Dad!"

Pat turned to her, his eyes uncharacteristically wide. "I heard Missy in here! Don't try to tell me I'm crazy. I heard it loud and clear!"

"It was just a voicemail, Dad." Ronnie held up her phone. She played the message again, and Pat's body slumped in disappointment.

"Why you messin' with me like that?"

"Dad, come on...you know Mama is dead. I'm not trying to mess with you; I wouldn't do that."

"What you call this? Playin' her voice where I can hear it?? This is my wife that I been missin' for twenty years and you gon' tease and play that in here? You tryin' to get back at me, ain't ya?"

He was losing it right in front of her, and Ronnie had to tell herself to stay calm. This was a tough time, for both of them.

She stood and went over to him, grabbing him by the shoulders.

"Dad. Look at me."

His chest heaving, Pat looked at her.

"You remember Aunt Debra telling you Mama passed, right?"

"Yeah..."

"Do you think she was lying to you?"

He paused. "No."

"So you know there's no way she could be in here, right?"

Pat paused. "I suppose."

Several quiet moments passed. "Still think you don't need to go to therapy?"

Pat glared at her, then averted his eyes.

Chapter 15

The day of the memorial service came quickly.

Pat got up early as usual. Made his bed, taking more care than usual in making sure it was just so. Then he headed to the kitchen to make breakfast. He could hear Ronnie up and moving around in her room as he passed by.

"They workin' on the roads so we gon' have to leave a little early," he muttered, arranging all of his ingredients. He was making grits, eggs, pancakes, cheese toast, and smoked sausage, way more than he usually made. "You don't like when I drive too fast, I know. I'll be sure to be careful, 'specially since they said it might rain."

He went about making his breakfast, continuing to talk as if someone else was in the room as he had gotten used to doing. His movements were fluid, his routine so well-oiled that it was effortless. At some point, Ronnie came and stood in the door of the kitchen, watching him, but he didn't notice. He just kept on cooking and talking. It wasn't until he was about done that Ronnie finally entered the room and began preparing her own breakfast. Neither of them said a word to each other, but Pat did stop talking to himself when Ronnie came in.

Ronnie knew pancakes were Missy's favorite breakfast. And when she saw Pat slice up an orange to eat with everything, she knew that this meal was in homage to Missy. Pat almost never ate fruit for breakfast, and she hadn't seen him make pancakes since she moved back home. He was making everything Missy liked.

When he was done eating, Pat wordlessly headed back to his room to get ready. Ronnie cleaned up the dishes before going to her room to do the same. Part of her was waiting for the ball to drop with Pat; he was too calm. She couldn't imagine he had come to grips with everything that happened recently already. They never discussed his freak-out over hearing Missy's voicemail a couple of nights before, but Ronnie could tell Pat was a little embarrassed by it. But she was anxious about how he would react when he got to the memorial.

Pat didn't want to go. Going to a memorial for his wife was like putting the nail in the coffin. Part of him had been imagining that she was still alive, off on her personal journey. It brought him comfort, even though he knew it wasn't smart or healthy. Missy was gone, dead, and he needed to accept that. It was the only reason he agreed to go to this memorial.

After he showered, he took extra care in getting dressed, wanting to look especially nice. He shaved slowly, careful not to nick himself. Missy used to always get onto him about his ashy knuckles, so he made sure to moisturize everything thoroughly. Spritzed on his good cologne that he had stopped bothering to wear. It was the cologne Missy had given him on the last anniversary they shared together.

His dark gray suit was already laid out. When he went to church, he usually just wore slacks and a button-down shirt with the occasional tie, but today he was going all out. This was not like any other day and he wasn't going to act like it was.

"Hope you like the suit," he muttered. He perused his appearance in the slightly-chipped mirror. "Haven't worn this thing in a while; surprised it still fits."

Ronnie stood near his door, which was uncharacteristically ajar. She noted the dress laid out neatly on the bed, with matching pumps just under it on the floor. One of Missy's favorite purses was on the bed, also.

"We're not gonna be late," Pat said. "I'll get us there on time. Promise."

Ronnie wordlessly walked away.

A little while later, Pat met her in the living room. She looked up at him and smiled tightly.

"Ready?" Pat looked at his watch.

"As ready as I'm going to get for this. Let's go."

Neither of them said much as they headed to the community center where the memorial was being held. Debra opted not to have it at their church, as she didn't want it to seem so formal. And Missy used to volunteer at the community center, so it seemed fitting to have it there.

The meeting room was set up with chairs and a podium. A small table with a few pictures of Missy was off to the side. There were no flowers or other decorations. No refreshments. There was a small radio playing soft jazz, which was Missy's favorite, but that was about it, as far as ambiance. Ronnie didn't know whether to appreciate the simplicity or be offended by it.

"I'm so glad you both decided to come," Debra greeted, giving them each warm hugs. "We're going to be getting started in just a few minutes."

"I didn't expect so many people to be here," Ronnie admitted, looking around the room. There were at least twenty people there. "I don't know why, though."

"Its several people from church, and some other family members."

No wonder I don't recognize them, Ronnie mused silently.

"They just want to pay their respects," Debra continued. She tucked her shoulder-length black hair behind her ear. "They've all asked about Missy over the years."

"How is this going to go? Is there a program or something?"

"No, not really. We'll start with a prayer and then whoever wants to can get up and speak about Missy. That's about it, really. I just want the people who need that closure to have it."

"This is gonna be tough," Ronnie predicted, a hand on her stomach. Pat still hadn't said anything.

"I know, baby." Debra put an arm around her niece. "I can't imagine what you must be feeling right now. Get up and speak or sit right in that chair; it's entirely up to you. I'm just thankful that you're here at all."

"Thanks, Aunt Debra."

"And you too, Pat," Debra turned to him. "My heart warmed when I saw you walk through that door. I'm not going to pretend to know how you're feeling. I just want us all to be here for each other during this difficult time as much as we can. Missy was a big part of keeping everyone together and when she left, a lot of people detached themselves."

"Including me," Ronnie mumbled.

"But family should be together," Debra proclaimed, grabbing Pat's forearm and gently pulling him closer. She noticed how he tensed, but didn't comment on it. "I know everyone had gotten used to doing their own thing, but I'd surely like for us to get to know each other better as a family and start really building that relationship."

Ronnie couldn't help but smile. Debra was as much of a sweetheart as Missy was.

"I'd like that, too," she said.

Pat just looked at the ground. The ladies peered at him, but didn't try to get him to respond. This was a tough day for him, and they both knew it. He couldn't be pushed.

Shortly after, Debra started the service. Of course, she had Ronnie and Pat sitting right up front. After saying a short prayer and thanking everyone for coming, she began recalling some stories from her and Missy's childhoods, most of which made everyone chuckle. Ronnie could tell Debra didn't want this to be a sad event. She was dressed in a tangerine wrap dress, and most of the guests were in things they might wear to a normal church service. Only Ronnie was dressed in black.

Guess I missed the memo on the vibe, she thought as she glanced around the room. Right before turning back around, she saw Tess slip into the room and take a seat in the back. Ronnie was touched that she showed up, especially since it was during prime salon business hours, and flashed her an appreciative smile.

"Missy never liked getting reprimanded so there were plenty of times she would blame things on me that I didn't do," Debra was saying. "But she always felt bad about it, and tried to make it up to me by giving me candy or her pork chop at dinner. She was just never very good at facing difficult situations. Confrontation always made her nervous, almost to the point of panicking. But her little sister being upset with her for a while was never a problem."

The room laughed. Everyone except Pat. Ronnie could only manage a tight smile.

"She really was a nice woman," Debra continued, her smile wistful. "My heart hurts today. It'll probably hurt for a while. But it's nice to remember the good things. There are plenty of wonderful memories I can wrap myself in when things get tough." She dabbed her eyes with the handkerchief in her hand and invited other people to come say a few words.

There was a steady stream of people who wanted to share their memories of Missy. Most of them were lighthearted and funny, or praiseworthy in nature. With every person that spoke, Ronnie learned something new about her mother. After several people's speeches, Ronnie began to realize she hadn't known Missy very well at all.

"There are a lot of good things about Missy that I remember," a man said, his hands gripping the side of the podium. Ronnie recognized him as Pastor Chambers, from their church. His tall frame hovered over the podium as he contemplated his next words. "A good number of them were already touched on by you all. There's something on my heart, though, that I was going back and forth about whether I was going to mention it or not. And I just don't feel its right to keep it to myself any longer."

Ronnie's ears perked up. Pat eyed his pastor curiously.

"Missy reached out to me a couple of years ago," Pastor Chambers announced. "Called me out of the blue, right before service one Sunday morning. She was in Atlanta, which she asked me to keep to myself."

Ronnie's mouth fell open. Her mother had come back? Pat and Debra looked equally shocked.

"She had been planning to come to service, because she was missing her family so much." Pastor Chambers looked at

Ronnie and Pat, his eyes remorseful. "She spoke a lot about both of you, and about how guilty she felt for leaving like she did. It was her biggest regret in life, she said. I urged her to go home, to make things right and explain herself, and she said she would. She *promised* she would; said enough time had passed."

The room was spinning. Ronnie grabbed for Debra's hand.

"There are several things she revealed to me during that call," Pastor Chambers continued. He dropped his head, clearly anguished. "She begged me to not tell anyone, that she was going to come clean on her own. Knowing she never did, that she left town again without another word to her family, makes me ashamed. Whenever I would look out into my congregation and see her husband or her sister sitting there, knowing I knew more than they did, it was like a kick in the gut. And I apologize to you both for that right now. And even though I haven't seen you in quite a while, Ronnie, this goes for you, too."

Pat's jaw was clenched as a tear streamed down his cheek. His breath became shallower. Ronnie grabbed his stiff hand in her free one, wondering if he was going to explode. Ronnie was so conflicted with confusion over what she was hearing that she almost couldn't see straight.

"I'll be happy to tell the three of you everything she said to me," Pastor Chambers said, looking right at Pat, Ronnie, and Debra. "I know now is not the venue, but whenever you're ready to hear it, just let me know."

Pastor Chambers took his seat, and everything was still for several moments. No one really knew what to say or do after his bombshell.

Finally, Ronnie made herself stand. Inching to the podium, she resisted the urge to run out of the room like she wanted to. Her body felt like it weighed a ton. Her eyes strayed to Tess, whose expression was clear concern.

"Do you wanna leave?" Tess mouthed.

She did. But Ronnie just slightly shook her head. She wasn't going to be a coward, like her mother clearly was.

"Um," she cleared her throat. "I'm not really sure how to follow that..."

She glanced at her Aunt Debra, who was rocking side to side with her hand on her chest. She was crying. Pat was just sitting here, looking at the floor, clearly still reeling from Pastor Chambers' revelation.

"For those of you who don't know, I'm Missy's daughter, Ronnie." She stood up a little straighter. "And I honestly wasn't sure if I was going to get up and say anything or not. I hadn't seen my mother in twenty years. There were so many times that I needed her and she wasn't here. I'm angry. I'm hurt. And after what I just heard..." She shook her head. "I honestly feel like I'm mourning a stranger."

There were a few sniffles around the room. Several people nodded understandably.

"I didn't really know what I was going to say before and I surely don't know what to say now," Ronnie continued. "My mother is dead, and as strange as it sounds, it's at least nice to know *that*. For years I didn't know anything. I always revered Missy Duncan, focusing on the good memories and making myself forget that there probably wouldn't be any more. Yes, she was a good woman, but she was also selfish. She left her family hanging without a word. And as much as I'd like to stand here and tell a pleasant story, all I can think about is how my mother left me when I needed her most. And that's probably how I'll always remember her."

Knowing the vibe in the room had been totally killed, Ronnie retook her seat.

The service ended shortly after that. Everyone knew there was nothing they could say to brighten Missy's image at that point, and that it would be disrespectful to try. They just hugged Ronnie, Pat, and Debra, threw out some encouraging words, and hastily filed out.

Tess hung back, asking Ronnie and Pat if they needed her to do anything. Ronnie introduced her to Debra, and Pat accepted Tess's hug, though he still wasn't speaking. Ronnie pulled Tess over to the side.

"I really appreciate you being here," she said. "I know it's probably busy at the salon right now, it being Saturday afternoon and all."

"Family comes first," Tess said immediately. "And I told you, y'all are family now. The rest of the girls wanted to be here, too, but they had to hold things down at the salon."

"Of course, yeah. Please thank them for me."

"I will. I'm not gonna bother asking if you're all right 'cause I know you're not. You probably feel like you're in the Twilight Zone right now."

"To put it mildly."

"Whatever you need, just let me know. Time off, a girls night out, someone to scream your head off to, some stiff drinks, whatever. If I can do it, you've got it."

Ronnie looked at Tess gratefully. She had no idea when she ran into her a few months back that she would become someone so important to her.

"I can't thank you enough, Tess." She placed a hand on her arm. "You've saved my bacon several times now."

Grinning at the reference, Tess placed a hand over hers. "There's been people that saved *my* bacon plenty of times, too. You don't keep that kind of goodwill to yourself."

To both her own and Tess's surprise, Ronnie lunged forward to give Tess a tight hug, needing it more than ever right then.

Ronnie drove Pat home, knowing he was in no condition to drive. He still hadn't said a word. Ronnie knew the hurt and shame he had been feeling all these years was on a rolling boil, but after hearing Pastor Chambers' news, Ronnie was just waiting for it to explode into a big scalding mess. He was eerily calm, too calm, and Ronnie was nervous. There was no telling when he was going to snap, and she was sure he would eventually.

As soon as they got home, Pat immediately went to his bedroom and pulled out a couple of suitcases. Ronnie stood at the door and watched as he began to pack Missy's things, carefully folding each item and packing them in the space-optimizing ways Missy taught him. He gathered any toiletries, pictures, photo albums, knickknacks, and anything else that belonged to Missy, and packed them away.

"Need any help?" Ronnie finally offered.

"No," Pat finally spoke. "I'm doin' this by myself."

When all of Missy's things were packed, Pat grabbed both suitcases, grunting slightly at their heft. Ronnie stepped aside as he stomped out of the room, determined. Ronnie thought he was going to put the suitcases in his truck, but to her surprise, he was heading straight for the backyard.

"Dad, what are you doing?" she asked as Pat dumped the suitcases by the back door and headed for the outside shed where he kept his lawn equipment and tools. Ronnie had forgotten the shed was back there.

Pat sprayed the middle of the yard with water, plunked down a few cinderblocks, then drug two metal barrels to put on top of them. He dumped a suitcase into each, then went back into the house, emerging with an armful of old newspapers. He stuffed them towards the bottom of the barrels, not caring at all that he was dirtying his suit. He then pulled a utility lighter from his pocket.

"Dad..."

Pat set all of Missy's things on fire. Ronnie rushed into the house for the fire extinguisher to have on hand, just in case. She returned to the backyard, scanning to make sure there weren't any power lines over the fire and glad there weren't any nearby bushes or trees. Pat clearly hadn't thought to check for that, but then again, he wasn't in his right mind and Ronnie knew it. So that was her job.

As the fire built, Pat just stood there and watched. Stood there sweating and heaving as the last of Missy's items went up in flames. The frown on his face was vengeful, but his eyes showed pleasure at the sight in front of him.

Ronnie came and stood beside him. She didn't even know how to feel right then. Part of her was upset about Pat burning Missy's things, then she wondered why that was, since she didn't have any particular attachment towards any of it. She could've asked to keep a memento if she wanted. But as she stood there, she realized she didn't want any of Missy's things. Letting Pat burn her belongings felt like an act of rebellion, which she felt perfectly justified in after learning what she learned today about Missy.

When she heard Pat sobbing, Ronnie turned to him, dropping the fire extinguisher. Pat hung his head and cried, loudly, the weight of everything coming down on him. He fell to his knees, and Ronnie quickly followed, wrapping her arms around him. She let him fall against her as he continued to cry, both of them sitting on the wet grass in their mourning attire, leaning on each other like they never have.

"I love you, Dad."

Chapter 16

After another week or so, Pat finally agreed to go to counseling.

Ronnie hadn't pressured him. She was starting to wonder if she still wanted to go, herself. But when Debra called to check on them, she reiterated how much therapy was helping her. Just in the week since Missy's memorial service, she had been to two sessions, needing extra help dealing with the new information she learned.

With Debra's help, Ronnie selected a family therapist and made an appointment for her and Pat. Even though Pat had agreed to go on his own, it didn't mean he was enthusiastic about it.

"Let's get this over with," he groused as they were preparing to leave.

"Dad, if you're going to have that kind of attitude about it, we might as well not even bother going."

"Don't expect me to be gung-ho about goin' to a shrink."

"It's a family therapist. And if you don't really want to go, why did you say you would?"

"'Cause I clearly can't trust my pastor like I thought so I figured this was the next best thing."

Ronnie looked at him sympathetically. She knew he was still reeling from Pastor Chambers' news because she was, too. She had gone back and forth many times between being angry with him and understanding the position he was in. And she still wasn't even sure that she wanted to know what Missy had told him that day.

She opted not to try to defend Pastor Chambers right then. They could hash it all out in therapy.

"Come on, Dad," she said, gently ushering him towards the door. "Let's go."

Dr. Odom welcomed them both with a smile. Ronnie liked her immediately because she gave off such a pleasant vibe. Her eyes were bright behind her glasses, which were on a chain. Ronnie guessed she was around sixty or so, with her face showing just a few wrinkles and mostly-gray hair that was pulled in a high bun. Her skin reminded Ronnie of creamed coffee.

"Welcome, both of you," Dr. Odom greeted. "I'm so glad you made it. Please come in."

Ronnie and Pat trudged into the small office, subtly taking in their surroundings. Cream-colored walls, a desk, a couch, a chair, bookshelves. The basics. It was simple but still had a hominess to it.

"So," Dr. Odom began after they exchanged minor pleasantries. She sat in the chair opposite the couch where Ronnie and Pat were, a legal pad in her lap. "Why don't you tell me what brings you here?"

Pat and Ronnie looked at each other, each wanting the other to speak up first. Several moments passed as they silently dueled.

Finally, Ronnie sighed. "My mother died recently."

"I'm so sorry to hear that. How did she pass?"

Ronnie looked to Pat, since she didn't know. Pat cleared his throat. "A stroke."

"Were you all close?"

"Hadn't seen her in twenty years. So 'parently not."

Dr. Odom's eyebrow arched slightly, and she made a note on her pad.

"That's a long time. Did something happen twenty years ago?"

"No."

"She just left without a word?"

"Pretty much."

"When was the last time you spoke to her?"

"Day before she left."

"Was it an argument?"

Pat shifted in his seat. He was getting agitated. "No."

Dr. Odom eyed him over her glasses before making another note. "Ronnie, how was your relationship with your mother?"

"It was good. Or so I thought."

"Why do you say that?"

"Because she left anyway."

"There weren't any hints or indications that she might've been unhappy?"

Pat grunted. Ronnie glanced at him before replying, "Not to me, no."

Dr. Odom continued to ask questions and Pat just sat there with his arms folded, already tired of it. He regretted coming here. What help could this doctor be when they didn't know anything about why Missy left?

And as he listened to Ronnie's answers, he got even more frustrated. She wasn't really saying much of anything. This was just like a long, irritating interview, and Pat just wanted to leave. He had no idea that Ronnie was equally as frustrated with him.

When their time was up, Dr. Odom encouraged them to come back the following week. Pat hurried out the door, while Ronnie apologized for her father's rudeness and thanked the doctor seeing them.

It didn't take long for the argument to start.

"That was a big ol' waste of time," Pat fussed. "If you wasn't gon' say nothin', we coulda just stayed home."

"Me??" Ronnie was incredulous. "You're the one that gave all the barely-there answers. Not to mention you clearly had an attitude. I bet Dr. Odom could see that."

"I don't care if she could see it. I answered what she asked me."

"Come on, Dad. You didn't elaborate on anything. We're never gonna get anywhere if she has to drag every little thing out of you."

"Don't act like you was some chatterbox yo'self, 'cause ya wasn't."

"At least I was trying! And I wasn't acting like that was the last place I wanted to be, like you were!"

"I went, didn't I?"

"Dad, if we're gonna do this, you have to start taking it more seriously."

"I'm plenty serious. But don't be gettin' onto me when you guilty of the same stuff."

Ronnie glared at him, then sucked her teeth. They didn't speak to each other for the rest of the ride home.

As soon as they were inside the house, they each went to their respective rooms, slamming the doors. Ronnie flung herself across the bed, emotionally exhausted. That certainly didn't go as well as she hoped. Pat had been his usual stubborn self; Ronnie didn't know why she had expected anything different. Ronnie wondered if she should just go to therapy alone, but knew that she had issues with Pat just like she had issues with Missy. Their father-daughter relationship had improved greatly, but that wasn't saying much because it was practically non-existent before.

After a while, Ronnie heard the front door close. Glancing at her watch, she noticed an hour had passed already. After laying around for a few more minutes, she rolled off the bed and changed into a t-shirt and shorts before shuffling to the living room. Checking outside, she saw that Pat had indeed left. Ronnie breathed a sigh of relief, thankful for the reprieve.

She headed to the kitchen, her stomach reminding her that she hadn't eaten in hours. Deciding she didn't feel like cooking anything, she pulled a frozen veggie pizza from the freezer and turned on the oven. She was searching the cabinets for a pan when there was a knock on the door.

"Who is it?" she called out.

"Uncle Alvin."

Ronnie froze. With everything that had been going on recently, she'd forgotten all about him. In that instant, she hated that Pat wasn't in the house.

"What do you want?"

"I heard about Missy and just wanted to come over and pay my condolences."

"Okay, thanks. Have a nice day."

"Ronnie. Can you open the door?"

"I don't see why that's necessary."

"Look...I get why you're upset with me. Let's talk about it."

Was he about to apologize for molesting her? Ronnie knew there was nothing he could possibly say to make up for everything he did. He'd been acting like nothing even happened.

"We don't have anything to talk about. Now please go away."

She turned to leave the room. Suddenly, the door opened. She whirled around. Pat must have forgotten to lock it behind him when he left. And now his twin brother was right in front of her.

"I see my brother still has his bad habits," Alvin commented. He closed the door behind him. "He used to forget to lock the door when we were kids, too. That's one thing we don't have in common."

Fear shot through Ronnie when she saw him lock the door, his eyes on her.

She tried to sound strong. "Look, I don't know what you think you're gonna do, but-"

"Sweetheart, please. I don't wanna hurt you." Alvin stepped towards her. "I've never wanted to hurt you."

"And I don't want to hear this. Please leave."

"I think we both know it's past time that we hashed things out."

"Nothing to hash out. If you're here for absolution, you're wasting your time."

"Ronnie." He took another step towards her. "You know I love you. Haven't I shown you that?"

Ronnie hated that she was so far away from her phone. She knew there was no way she could get to it without him catching her first. He was standing between her and the door. She could make a break for the back door, but she knew he'd probably catch her easily. Alvin had kept himself in great shape over the years, unlike Pat who had a slight paunch from all the beers and heavy foods he constantly enjoyed.

"What you've shown me is that you're a sick man who should be behind bars," Ronnie said, hating that her voice quivered.

Alvin stopped and looked around. He appeared to be listening for noise. "Where's Pat?"

Ronnie froze. She didn't want him to know she was there alone. "He's sleeping."

"I didn't see his truck outside."

"It's in the garage."

"He doesn't usually park in the garage."

"Well, he did today."

"You know what I think? I think it's just you and me here," Alvin surmised, advancing towards her. He smirked, making Ronnie's skin crawl. "We're finally alone again."

"I'm warning you," Ronnie pointed a finger at him, slowly walking backwards. She tried to sound strong, but she was clearly afraid. It was easy to be angry and tough when Pat was there. But now it was just her and her uncle, and she knew he could overpower her if he tried. "I'm not a little girl anymore. You can't just have your way with me like you used to."

"You're right. You're not a little girl. You've grown into a beautiful, sexy woman." Alvin licked his lips. "And you'll like it a lot more now that you're an adult. We both will."

"You're sick."

"No, I'm in love. Always have been."

"I'm your *niece*!"

"You're female. That's all that really matters, at the end of the day."

Ronnie's stomach lurched. She couldn't even believe she was related to this man.

"I'll scream."

"Go ahead; I like screams." He rubbed his hands together as he looked at her hungrily. "We're *both* gonna be screaming in a few minutes."

Ronnie's eyes scanned the room for anything she could use as a weapon. Unfortunately, anything that might've been of any use had been burned in the backyard. Ronnie hadn't even noticed how bare the room looked now that Missy's things were gone.

Desperate, she picked up the lamp and held it up near her head, as if she was about to throw and Aaron Rogers-worthy hail mary.

"Stay away from me!"

Alvin moved closer to her. "I've missed you."

"Get out!"

"No need in trying to fight it, baby. This is happening."

He was looking at her the way he used to look at her when she was a child. As soon as the door closed behind Missy and Pat when they would drop her off, Alvin's pleasant eyes and easygoing smile faded into a lustful stare and a devious smirk. And the older she got, the worse it got. After he took her virginity, he didn't bother with the pretense of ice cream or movies; as soon as they were alone, he was on her like white on rice. He only left her alone when he had gotten his fill. Ronnie would sit there, crying, as he fixed her something to eat as if he didn't have a care in the world. On the few occasions he indulged in a post-coital nap, Ronnie would stare at him, trying to work up the nerve to bash his head in with a hammer or pour hot grease on him. Now, she wished she had.

Ronnie thought about running towards the hallway, but that would be trapping herself since there were no exits in that part of the house. Tears stung her eyes. She couldn't believe this was happening again.

Well, if he wants to take it, he's gonna have to fight me for it.

Chucking the lamp at him, Ronnie made a beeline for the back door. The sudden movement surprised Alvin, and he ducked to avoid the lamp, but he recovered quickly. He caught Ronnie just before she reached the back door, grabbing and lifting her by the waist, pulling her back towards the living room kicking and screaming.

"*Take your hands off me!*" she yelled at the top of her lungs, clawing his arms like an alley cat.

"I see you've gotten feisty," Alvin said, clearly struggling with his flailing niece. He yelped when Ronnie kicked him hard in the shin. "Stop fighting me!"

Ronnie tried to twist out of his grasp, but his hold on her was too strong. He flung her to the couch, thwarting her immediate attempt to get up by bracing his hands on her shoulders. His hands grabbed her shirt collar, ripping it with little effort. He groped for her breasts, practically unfazed when she slapped him across the face. He was determined, and clearly not going to stop until he got what he wanted.

"God, you're beautiful," Alvin whispered amidst Ronnie's screams. He managed to work himself between her kicking legs, and she felt that familiar granite erection press against her. In that moment, she hated that she had on shorts. Alvin was already grinding his hips subtly, and years of forcibly-suppressed memories flooded Ronnie's brain like deadly wave. She was crying, but he didn't care.

"Please," she begged, hating herself for doing so. "Please stop!"

He caught both of her wrists, then held them with one hand above her head. She couldn't pry them free no matter how hard she tried; it was like they were in a vice grip. The tears streamed harder. He had her pinned with his hard body, vulnerable, and she was realizing there wasn't much she could do about it. Her strength was waning, and he knew it was only a matter of time before she physically couldn't fight him anymore.

Alvin leaned down to kiss her, but she whipped her head from side to side, trying to bury her face in the sofa cushion. Alvin removed the cushion with his free hand and tossed it to the floor before forcibly holding her face still and pressing his lips against hers. Ronnie squeezed her eyes shut, disgusted, and tried to prevent his tongue from entering her mouth. His hand was now trying to work its way in between them, roughly fondling her. Ronnie tried to scoot and squirm, anything to disrupt him, but nothing worked. Wherever she moved, he moved.

He was struggling to unzip his pants while running the flat of his tongue across her mouth and chin, lapping at her face like an ice cream cone. His licks were slow and long. Ronnie winced as his super-hard erection repeatedly pressed against her, his body burrowing hers into the worn sofa.

"Give it up," he panted, his hot breath searing her face. "I've got you."

"Never," Ronnie said through gritted teeth.

She was getting tired. It would be so easy to just lay there and let him get his rocks off. But she wasn't a kid anymore; unlike back then, she knew what he was doing was wrong. And she knew she didn't deserve this. So she would try to fight him off for as long as she could.

"I can't wait to get inside of you again," he whispered, sucking hard on her neck. "We've got a *lot* of time to make up for."

Ronnie tried to crane her neck away, her mind racing as to how she could possibly get out of this. Her feet hadn't stopped kicking at him, but this only seemed to spurn him on. Her screams seemed pointless. So Ronnie did the only thing she could do; pray for some kind of intervention.

"You are not gonna get away with this," she cried. "I told my dad about what you did to me."

"And you see he didn't do anything about it," Alvin retorted smugly. "I told you; he doesn't care."

He yanked her bra aside and grabbed her breast, squeezing and admiring it for a quick moment before ducking his head to take it into his mouth. When he did this, he slid his body down slightly, and his grip on her wrists loosened just enough for her to pry free. Ronnie immediately started pounding his head with her fists, her strength renewing.

"Help!" she screamed as Alvin tried to capture her wrists again. She prayed a neighbor or someone else outside would hear her. "*Somebody please help me!!*"

"Ronnie?"

The doorknob jiggled. Relief washed over Ronnie, and Alvin looked panicked. He tried to cover her mouth with his hand, but Ronnie hurled her body towards the floor, both of them landing with a loud thump. It didn't register to her who might be at the door that would know it was her inside; it sure wasn't Pat's voice, and besides, he had a key.

"I'm being attacked! Please help!" she screamed towards the door.

"Shut up!" Alvin bellowed, becoming angry. He grabbed a handful of her braids and yanked her head back as she tried to squirm away. "You shut up right now!"

"What's going on in there?!"

Ronnie knew that voice, but it couldn't be. There was no way.

"Edward??"

There were several hard bangs on the door before it flew open, and Edward charged into the room.

"What the hell?" His eyes surveyed what was going on, hardening when he noticed Ronnie's torn shirt. Before Ronnie could blink, Edward was on Alvin, punching him so hard that blood shot out of his mouth onto the carpet. Ronnie scurried away, righting her bra. She was still trying to process seeing Edward right in front of her after no contact for months.

"So you tryin' to rape my wife?" Edward growled as he continued to pummel Alvin's face. "You tryin' to rape my *wife*?"

His wife?

Ronnie's head was swimming. Alvin showing up, attacking her, and then Edward busting in like an action hero and beating Alvin like a villain was throwing her for a major loop, and she sincerely began to wonder if this was all some kind of dream. Had she dozed off after coming home from therapy? Had she even *gone* to therapy? She placed a hand against her throbbing head, wondering if she was losing her mind.

"What in the world??" Pat exclaimed. He was standing in the doorway, looking totally mortified.

Ronnie hurried over to him and threw her arms around his neck. The tears immediately came back and words just started spewing. "Uncle Alvin said he was coming by to pay his condolences for Mama, and then he just walked in 'cause you forgot to lock the door again and when he realized you weren't here he attacked me and was raping me and then Edward showed up and heard him and broke down the door and started beating him up—"

"He tried to rape you??"

"He didn't *try*. That's what he was doing!"

"Who is this man in here beatin' him up?"

"That's Edward. My...ex-husband."

Pat looked at her, but didn't take the time to ask for more details. He just dropped the Wal-Mart bag in his hand and told Ronnie to call the police.

"Move outta the way," Pat said to Edward in a voice Ronnie didn't recognize, pushing him aside. He grabbed his bloodied, barely-conscious twin brother by the collar and picked him up with strength Ronnie didn't even know he had.

"That's my daughter." His voice was menacing. "You put yo' hands on my *daughter*?"

"She's lying," Alvin breathed, his eyes half-open. He grasped Pat's shirt. "I'm your twin brother. She's lying on me."

"Oh my gosh!" Ronnie cried. Edward had already come over to comfort her, and he wrapped his arms tighter around her.

"It's okay, baby...he won't be hurting you again. I *promise*," he assured her, his lips against her temple. Ronnie clung to him, gripping handfuls of his shirt in her hands.

"My *daughter*," Pat said again. His hands clamped around Alvin's throat and began to squeeze. "She's all I got. Don't you *ever* think I love you more than I love her, and you betta believe that just as sure as you believe in Jesus! That's my daughter. My *daughter*!"

"Auugh!" Alvin clawed at Pat's hands, his eyes bulging in fear. He could see the look in his brother's eyes; his curled lip, his cheeks quivering with intensity, literally turning red from rage. "Pat...I can't breathe..."

"I know you can't breathe. That's why you choke folks, so they can't breathe."

"Dad..." Ronnie finally cautioned after several moments of enjoying what he was doing. She gently eased from Edward's embrace and slowly walked over to Pat, placing her hands on his arms. "Dad. Don't do this. Let the police handle it."

"I care what happens to ya," Pat stressed, glancing at her. His hands were still squeezing his brother's throat. "I believe everything you said he did."

"I know, Dad. I know you do." Ronnie looked at her uncle, who was starting to lose consciousness. As much as she enjoyed watching him suffer, she couldn't let her father be responsible for ending his life. Even if he deserved it. "He'll get what's coming to him. There's no way he can lie himself out of this. Please, let God and the police deal with him."

Pat didn't want to let God and the police handle it. He wanted to be the one to punish his brother. He had to make up for all the times he took Ronnie to Alvin's house only for Alvin to molest her.

"Dad..." Ronnie squeezed his arm. "We can't work on our relationship if you're behind bars. Please."

After several more moments, Pat reluctantly released his hold on Alvin's neck. Alvin fell to the floor, grabbing his neck and coughing hard.

Shortly after, the police arrived. As Edward explained to them what happened, Pat leaned close to Alvin, looking right into his eyes.

"I'm ashamed you my brother. The *only* reason I don't kill you dead is 'cause of her." He motioned his head towards Ronnie. "The same woman you was rapin' just saved yo' life. But I pray to high heaven somebody finishes the job when you behind bars."

Chapter 17

"**I** still can't believe all this."

Dr. Odom looked at Ronnie over her glasses. "What can't you believe, Ronnie?"

"*Any* of this. My uncle attacking me again...actually saying he's *in love* with me? My dad almost killing him. I've never, ever seen my father get that angry; not even the time I accidentally kicked over the good TV right before the World Series. And he was good and mad at that. Edward being back in my life..."

"How do you feel about that? Edward being back in your life?"

"I'm not sure how to feel about it," Ronnie admitted. She scratched her head, still not quite used to her signature braids being gone. Her short natural hair would take some getting used to. Tugging on her Atlanta Braves t-shirt, she looked up at the ceiling thoughtfully. "I've missed him, of course. But I had become so focused on getting my life together and working on my relationship with Dad that I didn't allow myself to think about him that much. I figured he was done with me."

"Why did he show up at your house that day?"

"He said he just had a gut feeling that something was wrong, and wanted to check on me." Ronnie smiled wistfully. "He got the shock of his life seeing me being raped. I never told him about how Uncle Alvin used to molest me."

"Why is that?"

"Ashamed, I guess. Embarrassed. Figured I deserved it."

"You felt like you deserved to be molested?"

"I figured there had to be a reason my parents kept leaving me over there with him. And since he was the adult, at first I thought he just knew better than I did. My parents never talked to me about sex or what to look out for, the do's and don'ts, any of that. I knew nothing."

Pat looked down at his hands guiltily.

"Are you angry with your parents for this?" Dr. Odom asked, scribbling on her pad.

"I was for years. And a small part of me still is, really. But the bigger part of me is angry for my mother going away and leaving us for years without a word. My dad stuck around. And I truly believe he didn't know anything about what his brother was doing to me."

"What about him resenting you for being a girl? How are you feeling about that?"

"I mean, I don't love it. I know some parents would prefer to have one gender over another but usually, they love whatever they get."

"Do you think your father didn't love you?"

Ronnie glanced at Pat thoughtfully. "I think he did. I just don't think he knew how to show it."

Pat and Ronnie had started going to therapy regularly since Alvin's attack on Ronnie. As angry as Pat had been that day at his brother, after the dust settled, he had a hard time coming to grips with seeing his twin being pulverized by the ex son-in-law he had never met because he had been raping his daughter in his house. That very night he began having nightmares, because it took him back to how he met Missy: coming to her rescue when she was getting beaten behind the local juke joint. All because she didn't want to dance with the guy. Pat saved her, nursed her, comforted her, and they fell in love. Got married a month later. And Pat was fine with it just being the two of them. But Missy wanted a child, and Pat didn't have the heart to refuse her. And when they found out they were having a girl, Pat knew he was in trouble.

"I didn't," Pat agreed softly. "But I'm trying now."

"I know you are, Dad." Ronnie rubbed his back.

It was tough for both of them to open up, but the more they did, the more they both learned about each other. Neither of them went back to ask Pastor Chambers about what it was Missy told him that day she showed up n Atlanta.

"Why don't you want to know?" Dr. Odom asked them in another session.

"I'm just not sure I want to hear it," Ronnie admitted. "Besides that, I can't imagine what reason she could have that would justify her up and leaving her family high and dry like she did."

"And for me, I just don't need no more surprises," Pat spoke up. "There's already too much I'm tryin' to deal with as it is. And if it's somethin'...bad...well, I just wanna hang onto what good memories I can."

"How are you feeling about Missy's passing now, Pat? Any differently?"

"Feel a lil' guilty."

"Guilty? Why?"

"Because I'm relieved she's gone," he admitted. "I been hangin' onto hope for over twenty years. Every day, hopin' I'd see her walk through the door. Or at least get a phone call. All I ever got from her were some postcards."

Ronnie's head snapped to him. "Postcards? What postcards?"

Pat forgot Ronnie didn't know anything about that. "Missy would send them to Debra every now and again, just to let us know she was all right. Debra would give 'em to me when I went to church."

"How come you never told me about this?"

"We wasn't exactly on speakin' terms most of the time. And when you moved back to the house, we just each kinda minded our own business. I only got a couple of 'em since you moved in, anyway. Guess I just never thought about it."

"I can understand that. Sharing with each other was never our strong suit."

"Do you still have the postcards, Pat?" Dr. Odom asked.

"Nope. Burned 'em. They never said much of anything, anyway."

"So you feel guilty because of the relief you feel after Missy's passing?"

"Yeah. All that time I felt obligated to wait for her."

"Did you want to move on with your life? See other women, maybe?"

Pat gave a quick glance towards Ronnie before looking at the ground. "Once or twice. Kinda. A lil' bit. But I never did nothin'."

"Pat, it's perfectly natural for you to feel that way."

"Yeah, Dad. You don't have to feel bad about that," Ronnie added.

"Well, there was this one thing..." Pat mumbled.

"What one thing?"

"Me and Debra...she, um, she kissed me one time."

Ronnie's eyes bugged, then she broke out into a grin. "Whaaat? You and Aunt Debra?"

"There ain't no *me and Aunt Debra*," Pat quickly clarified. "She had me over for dinner after church and when I was 'bout to leave, she did it. It didn't mean nothin'."

"Did you enjoy the kiss, Pat?" Dr. Odom asked.

Pat shifted in his seat, clearly uncomfortable. "I didn't hate it."

"I think Aunt Debra would be good for you, Dad," Ronnie mused. "She's a sweetheart, and she knows what it's like to lose her mate so you wouldn't have to worry about her doing anything like what Mama did. She'd take good care of you."

"I can take care of myself."

"There's nothing wrong with sharing your life with someone."

"What about you, Ronnie?" Dr. Odom asked. "What about sharing *your* life with someone?"

"Who knows." Ronnie eyed her wiggling foot.

"Is Edward officially back in the picture? Have you two discussed getting back together?"

"Not really. We *have* been talking, though, and I've told him things that I should've told him years ago, before we got married. And he shared some things with me, as well. It made me realize how little we actually communicated. No wonder we fell apart."

"Perhaps now that you two are communicating, you can slowly rebuild your relationship."

"Yeah, maybe. I certainly miss Edward. But I just want to be sure it would be because I really want to be with him and not because I feel indebted to him for saving me that day. And besides, I've still got a lot of affection issues."

"Well, we can certainly work on those, too."

"I don't need to be in here for that part," Pat quickly spoke up. Both Ronnie and Dr. Odom laughed.

"Well, while you're still in here," Dr. Odom said after she composed herself, "Let's talk about how things are going between you and Ronnie at home."

"Things are fine."

"Just fine? Have you been doing those communication exercises I suggested?"

"We do 'em. I feel silly, though."

"As long as you're sincerely putting forth the effort, that's the important thing. I'd really like to see you both continue to work on your relationship with each other."

Ronnie glanced at Pat, then looped her arm through his and rested her head on his shoulder.

"So would I."

About the Author

Jessica Terry lives in Douglasville, GA with her son, and loves cranking out more books. Connect with her on social media; she loves hearing from her readers. You can also sign up for her newsletter at www.jessicaterry.com[1] (and get a freebie, too).

If you enjoyed this story, please consider leaving a review!

Instagram: @authorjessicaterry

Twitter: @ItsJessicaTerry

Facebook: facebook.com/AuthorJessicaTerry

TikTok: @AuthorJessicaTerry

---

1. http://www.jessicaterry.com

Also from Jessica Terry:

Some Like 'em *Thick*
It's All Right...Now
Not By a Long Shot
Get Right
Decisions and Consequences
Take One For the Team
When You Share Too Much
Backtalk
Emasculated
Restless
Always and Nevers
She is Me
Split By the Bell
The Karma Call
Forehead Kiss

The Introvert Series